The Odessa Raid

Wingman 19

Books by Mack Maloney

Mack Maloney's Haunted Universe
Iron Star
Thunder Alley

Starhawk *series*
Starhawk
Planet America
The Fourth Empire
Battle at Zero Point
Storm Over Saturn

Chopper Ops *series*
Chopper Ops
Zero Red
Shuttle Down

Strikemasters *series*
Strikemasters
Rogue War
Fulcrum

Storm Birds *series*
Desert Lightning
Thunder from Heaven
The Gathering Storm

The Odessa Raid

Wingman 19

Mack Maloney

SPEAKING VOLUMES, LLC
NAPLES, FLORIDA
2019

The Odessa Raid

ISBN 978-1-64540-101-8

For my friend, Clancy Miller

PART ONE

The Secret Island

Chapter One

The Russians knew they were coming.

The United Americans . . .

Eight fighter-bombers, flying at 40,000 feet; speed 450 knots. A *Voronezh* long-range radar first picked them up crossing over the top of Norway.

Now they were heading east.

Their target was obvious: *Sekret Ostrov*, literally, the secret island. Hugging the southern tip of the Novaya Zenlya archipelago just off western Siberia, it was the site of the Vlex Shipyard, a place that had birthed the colossal *Admiral Isakov* aircraft carrier and the dreaded *Sun Bomba*, a nuclear-tipped missile whose flash was so bright it could blind millions in a mere second.

But the secret island was also known for something else: It was the Arctic headquarters for the world's most notorious war criminal, Viktor Viktorovich Robotov.

Alerted to the incoming air raid, the shipyard's defenders went to battle stations, though some wondered if the report was real.

Sekret Ostrov was the perfect hiding place. The shipyard was veiled not just by the endlessly brutal Siberian weather, but also by a mammoth, saw-toothed, crescent-shaped mountain that bordered it on three sides. Even on rare sunny days, the secret base was hidden by the shadows of this 1,000-foot peak. During the long polar nights, it was virtually invisible.

But there was nothing else within a thousand miles that the Americans would have flown halfway around the world to attack.

And now they were just 200 miles away and coming fast.

The shipyard had its own air force. Sixteen MiG-29 jet fighters, half of them always out on the runway, warmed up and ready to scramble at the first sign of trouble. Some of the best mercenary pilots in the New Russian Empire flew for Vlex Vklyuchennyy Inc. It was now time to earn their pay.

The first four MiG-29s launched immediately. Big, fast, twin-engine fighters, they were painted in all-white polar camo and loaded for bear. Lifting off in pairs, they went straight up, quickly accelerating to 500 knots. They needed to get to 20,000 feet fast; it was the best tactical position to be in when the attackers arrived.

Yet, just as the first two MiGs neared the top of the jagged mountain, both exploded in flames. Two loud bangs, two huge puffs of smoke, and then nothing but twin clouds of debris.

Flying right on their tails, the second pair of scramble jets tried desperately to veer away from the fiery wreckage. But it didn't make any difference. They also exploded in midair.

It all happened so fast that the four remaining scramble MiGs had already taken off, unaware of what was happening above them. They, too, went straight up on afterburner. They, too, blew up just as they passed the top of the mountain, their explosions so concussive they created avalanches all along the jagged peaks walling in the hidden base.

Those on the ground who saw all this were stunned.

Half of the secret island's air force was gone, just like that.

Catfish Johnson usually didn't mind the cold—but this was crazy.

He and his special-ops artillery unit known as the Righteous Brothers had fought in many places around the globe. But at 10 below zero, with the Arctic wind and snow blowing at 70 knots, *Sekret Ostrov* was by far the worst.

The Brothers were experts in handling the powerful 75-millimeter M-6 field gun, moving them in pieces, via pure muscle power when necessary, to some of the most unusual battlefields imaginable. They had perfected the drill of assembling, firing, and then disassembling their big guns, all in minutes. They were so good at it no other merc artillery outfit in the world even came close.

But for this mission, the Brothers were working with a new weapon: the British-made Javelin portable missile battery. Dropped off on the southern end of the secret island twelve hours before, they'd climbed the 1,000-foot sawtooth mountain carrying the pieces of two Javelin launchers, plus missiles, on their backs. Once on top, they built a small, hidden emplacement on the tip of a precarious ledge overlooking the vast Russian base below.

The task facing Johnson and his twenty-two-man team was simple—on paper, anyway. When the American strike force finally showed up on radar and the base's scramble jets took off to confront them, the mountaintop Javelins should blow the Russians out of the sky. But the team could carry only eight missiles up the side of the sheer, jagged cliff. There would be no spares. They'd needed every shot to count.

As it turned out, the Brothers went eight for eight. Once done, they took a moment to look down at the secret airbase. Even through the wind and blowing snow, it was clear the place was in a state of chaos. Air raid sirens howling, fires burning, avalanches still going off everywhere. Losing the eight scramble jets was a huge shock to the system.

But the Brothers could not enjoy the view for very long.

Now they had to climb back down.

The operations bunker for the secret base was built into the south side of the sawtooth mountain.

Just like outside, confusion reigned within. Dozens of red warning lights were flashing; dozens of TV monitors, radio transmitters and radar scopes were blinking madly. Klaxons were blaring in the background nonstop.

Nearly a hundred people worked in the bunker. Its gigantic picture window allowed them to look out on the shipyard, the air base, and the polar landscape beyond—which meant they'd had a front-row seat to what just happened. In fact, tiny pieces of the eight MiGs were still fluttering down on the base, looking very much like black snow.

A large radar screen dominated one wall of the control bunker. On it were the images of the eight American attackers, heading right for them. But the raiders were still five minutes away—and no other enemy warplanes were in the area.

So how were the scramble jets shot down?

*****

Looking down on it all from a balcony ten feet above the control room floor were the three senior officers in charge of *Sekret Ostrov*. A typical Russian command troika, their job was twofold: safeguard the shipyard, but more important, whenever he was in town, protect the man who built this place: Viktor Robotov.

The three commanders were not Russian military, not exactly. Everyone at the base was a mercenary, a paid member of Viktor's vast private army, which these days rivaled the real Russian military in size. However, no one at *Sekret Ostrov* was without sin, right down to the aircraft monkeys and the cooks. War crimes, mass rapes, and wanton murder—to be assigned here, one had to be as bad as the boss himself, if that was possible.

Debris from the eight doomed airplanes continued to fall as the three commanders, after a loud, contentious discussion, made a hasty announcement over the bunker's intercom: How were their comrades' aircraft so suddenly destroyed?

Dolzhno byt, oni stolknulis s amerikanskimi krylatymi raketami, otpravlennymi v kachestve prelyudii k vozdushnoy atake was the static-filled message to those below.

They must have collided with American cruise missiles, sent as a prelude to an air attack.

This was wildly wrong, and would have ramifications in the days to come. But at the moment, those in the bunker suddenly forgot about the demise of the eight MiGs. They were facing another crisis.

As seen on the big TV screen, one of the American airplanes was pulling ahead of the oncoming attack force. It had gone supersonic and was now plummeting from 40,000 feet, corkscrewing wildly, its wings overloaded with ordnance.

Pulling out of the vicious dive, the aircraft leveled off at 200 feet and began a roller coaster path toward *Sekret Ostrov*. It would drop off the radar screen, only to pop up somewhere else a few seconds later—and then disappear again. This made it impossible to get a lock on it.

Everyone in the bunker knew what was going on back in America. Not just that its fragmented military had suddenly regained superpower status, but that its mythical hero and leader, thought to be dead ten years now, had mysteriously reappeared and was the driving force behind the American resurgence.

Eyes glued to the big radar screen, no one in the bunker dared whisper his name. But they all knew it very well.

Krylo Chelovek
The Wingman.
No one else could fly like that.

All this happened in a matter of seconds. No sooner had the eight MiGs been blown out of the sky when the shipyard's substantial ground defense systems went hot.

A dozen anti-aircraft gun batteries ringed the base, both manned and automatically controlled. They were augmented by three SA-2 surface-to-air missile sites located at the far end of the runway. This was enough hardware to protect a small city. By numbers alone, it seemed impossible that an enemy could fly within five miles of the place.

Still, the order from the bunker to the base's anti-aircraft crews was blunt: No matter who was flying the incoming airplane, it *had* to be shot down.

Finally getting a radar lock on the intruder, three SAMs launched simultaneously, one from each site. The people in the bunker followed the missile tracks as they headed straight for the United American aircraft just entering the five-mile kill-zone. But at the last second, the airplane, once again flying at 200 feet but still going supersonic, began spinning wildly, wing over wing. The bizarre maneuver created an even larger radar signature around the jet fighter, giving the SAMS an even bigger target to aim for.

But incredibly, the three missiles reached the detonation point at the same moment, only to find their target had roller-coasted again and was nowhere in sight. The three SAMs collided instead, creating a massive fireball and explosion.

Meanwhile, clawing itself back up from a near-suicidal *fifty feet* in altitude and no longer spinning, the attacking jet flew right through the conflagration and kept coming at the base.

Now the air above *Sekret Ostrov* was filled with exploding anti-aircraft shells, fired both manually and automatically. The guns looked like firehoses spraying out vast streams of luminous red tracers. Yet the bunker's radar screen showed the lone attacking airplane was performing even more-uncanny maneuvers that took it up, over, and around the torrents of the crimson AA rounds.

Nothing could stop it.

At one mile out, the plane launched four weapons all at once. The bunker's defense systems identified them as KH-28 anti-radiation missiles, blockbusters that carried huge 350-pound high-explosive warheads. Everyone in the bunker knew they were heading right for them, attracted by their control room's massive radar system.

And there was nothing anyone could do about it, simply because no one ever thought an intruder would ever get this far.

"Hawk Hunter!" one of the commanders finally cried into his microphone, speaking the name no one else wanted to say. "American bastard . . ."

The four missiles hit the bunker a moment later.

A moment after that, Hawk Hunter—the Wingman— arrived over the shipyard.

He was flying his Su-34VLR naval attack jet on full afterburner, going 1,100 knots and still just 200 feet off the deck. They were still shooting at him, so he continued to weave his way through the AA bursts and the blowing snow, fully utilizing the big plane's speed and maneuverability, while hoping he wouldn't zig when he should have zagged.

Another trio of SA-2s was fired at him. This happened just as he passed through the smoke cloud billowing out of the burning command bunker. The SAMs were coming at him so quickly, the smart thing would have been to pull back, go straight up, bury the throttles, and outrace them.

But Hunter was here for a reason, one even bigger than taking out the mountainside bunker. He had to fly over the shipyard's harbor and take a quick infrared video of what was happening below. What it revealed might be the key to the whole attack.

He pushed the plane's stick hard right and swallowed about nine G's. When he could see clearly again, he was out over the island's icy harbor, heading for the ship-yard's repair docks.

A quick look over his shoulder told him two of the pursuing SAMs were beginning to spiral out of control, their guidance systems confused by his mind-bending flying. The third missile followed him for another few seconds, but it just couldn't keep up. Fuel expended, mo-tors shutting down, it crashed into the frigid waters be-low.

In the next second Hunter was over the inner harbor. He hit his FLIR-record button, starting the plane's infra-red video cameras whirring. It was all over in five sec-onds—that's all he needed.

He finally put the Su-34 on its tail and went straight up, creating an immense sonic boom and triggering even more landslides.

Many of the shipyard's AA guns had turned on their targeting radars when they fired at Hunter's crazily fly-ing plane. This was a fatal mistake—and also part of the Americans' plan.

No sooner had Hunter departed when two more Su-34s appeared out of the blowing snow. They launched another, larger barrage of KH-28 anti-radiation missiles, this time eight in all.

Each missile found a target by homing in on one of those radars that went hot trying to keep up with Hunter's jet. The fusillade destroyed nearly all of the automated and manned AA sites surrounding the secret base. Those guns that remained kept firing at the attackers, but the two planes were up and over the sawtooth range and gone in a flash.

It was only then that many at the secret base realized they were being attacked by warplanes made in Russia. They were all Su-34 VLR naval fighter jets, the former air arm of the *Admiral Isakov*, a vessel that had been built here, yet now was in possession of the Americans along with all its air squadrons. The big jet fighters were wearing the cool-blue sea camo patterns, but their wings and fuselages were emblazoned with the unmistakable emblem of the United States of America.

Another Su-34 suddenly roared over. It was carrying four American-made GBU-10 Paveway bombs. Designed to penetrate two feet into any surface before detonating, they were ideal for blowing up runways. Common sense said that at this point in the attack, destroying the shipyard's airstrip and stranding the eight remaining MiG-29s would be a lot easier than shooting them down.

The snowy, freezing cold air was still full of blazing AA shrapnel, but the plane managed to deliver its penetrator bombs perfectly, laying them right down the middle of the air strip, knocking it out of commission. Then it, too, disappeared over the mountain.

That was it. The first phase of the American air raid was now complete. It had lasted just fifty-five seconds, and so far, all of the attacking airplanes had survived.

But there was still one more thing to do.

Hunter leveled out at 20,000 feet.

He anxiously flipped the FLIR display button and slaved its output to his helmet's HUD visor. After a burst of static, the IR video focused and he could clearly see the results of his quick-cam snatch of the enemy base's inner harbor.

Eight warships were docked there. Three battle cruisers, three missile destroyers, two armed patrol boats—and one enormous black submarine.

Hunter banged his fist in triumph. It was the *Odessa*, code name for Viktor Robotov's super submarine.

This was what they had really come for.

He grabbed his radio mic and clicked it madly. Twenty, thirty times.

Everyone in the strike force knew what that meant.

A half mile down the strait that led to the shipyard, another gigantic submarine was lying in wait, its conning tower just barely breaking the surface of the freezing water.

It was the USS *Fitz*.

Nearly two football fields long and weighing close to 20,000 tons, it was an Ohio-class boomer that Hunter's close friend, Mike Fitzgerald, had been able to acquire and turn into his own underwater flagship, à la Jules Verne.

The *Fitz* was packed with the best weapons money could buy. Cruise missiles, high explosive torpedoes, armed drones. He even had a small army of Irish mercenaries on board, giving the sub its own marine corps. Added all up, the USS *Fitz* had more firepower than many countries around the world.

An Irishman with money can be a dangerous thing, and Fitz certainly was that. True-blue patriot and ever the businessman, he prowled the oceans hunting down anyone who would screw with his beloved adopted country, the USA.

At the moment, his crew was picking up the last of Catfish Johnson's men from the same rocky beach where they'd dropped them off hours before. Boarding rubber rafts just as soon as they rappelled back down the side of the sawtoothed mountain, the Brothers were quickly hustled aboard the *Fitz*.

The giant sub then launched an armed recon drone and submerged once again.

The waiting game began.

Fitz had been hunting Viktor for what seemed like forever.

But today, he was certain he had the devil trapped. Not only had Fitz's vast intelligence network confirmed the exact location of *Sekret Ostrov*, his spies had also uncovered its most glaring flaw. The whole thing—the shipyard, the air base and the harbor—sat on a colossal slab of Arctic ice. This made a perfect foundation for the airbase and the shipyard's weapons plants, but the manmade harbor had to be carved out, block by block. In doing so, its builders had created a huge basin.

There was only one channel in and out of this gigantic ice bowl. It ran north to south, emptied into the Kara Sea, and was usually storm-tossed and plagued by violent tides. And at the moment, the USS *Fitz* was blocking its approach.

There was more triumphant fist pounding when Hunter's message reached the sub's control room.

Lucifer was indeed up here, at the top of the world, visiting his frozen hell.

And if the air raid didn't get him, as soon as the super villain tried to make his escape, Mike Fitzgerald would.

The final wave of American attackers arrived; the second phase of the air raid had begun.

They were the strike force's refueling ships, four of them, known as buddy tankers. In addition to lugging two 1,200-gallon refueling pods each, they were also carrying APR-3E *Viyuga* aerial torpedoes.

These were smart weapons. Once dropped, the torpedo would circle underwater, looking for an appropriate target. When one was locked in, the torpedo would come to life, activate its warhead, and launch itself directly into its prey. Few survived such an attack in the open seas. If you were at anchor or docked, there was virtually no chance of escape.

Screaming down from 20,000 feet, Hunter led the buddy tankers in over the target area, flying just in front of them, firing his cannons at any hint of opposition. The armed tankers turned as one, dove to just 100-feet, and began a sweep across the secret island's large inlet bay. Each plane dropped its two torpedoes . . .

This was now the most important part of the raid. Parked front and center in the shipyard's main dock was

Viktor's super-sub, the *Odessa*. All of the torpedoes had been programmed to hit the enormous U-boat. If any other Russian warships got in the way that was the bad breaks of war. For the United American air crews, the devil's submarine was the prime target.

Yet, at the same moment the torpedoes hit the water, the shipyard's docks became enveloped in a thick, red mist, as if someone had lit off hundreds of pressurized paint canisters. The smoke and snow swirling around the shipyard was dense to begin with; the crimson fog made seeing the enemy sub extremely difficult.

Hunter flew right over the U-boat's location. Flipping down his night vision goggles, he was just in time to see the submarine disappear amid the confusion and smoke.

But was it sinking?

Or simply submerging?

In the next moment, a series of explosions erupted from the icy water. Russian warships were being hit—and sunk—but no one, including Hunter, could tell which ones.

This was *not* how they planned it. They needed validation that the torpedoes had hit Viktor's sub.

The rest of the attack force was now orbiting at 5,000 feet above the secret island. Hunter messaged them to get as many eyes as possible on the situation in the harbor.

This meant each airplane should engage its FLIR systems and scan the icy waters below looking for any evidence of battle damage to the *Odessa.*

Then he put his fighter into another gut-wrenching high-speed turn out over the water again and turned back toward the burning secret base. They'd come too far for this to be the flip of a coin. He was determined to keep buzzing the shipyard's harbor until he saw definite proof that the *Odessa* had been hit and was in the process of sinking.

But then . . . something else happened. His hands and feet started shaking. A buzz began bouncing between his ears. His five senses seemed to explode.

In the next moment, his entire being was vibrating.

He knew what this meant.

Keying his chin mic, and as calmly as possible, he said: "Strike—go vertical, full military power."

No matter where they were over the island, on Hunter's words, the other American pilots immediately pulled straight up and went to afterburner.

Then, with just a little more urgency, Hunter added: "Engage welders . . ."

The *Sun Bomba* nuclear warhead went off a moment later. It came out of the side of the sawtooth mountain, just below the already devastated command bunker. It blew away half of the secret island, the blinding mushroom cloud rising above the storm of ice shards suddenly blasted for miles in every direction.

The Americans had spent hours drilling for this. That the air strike might detonate one of Viktor's sun bombs had always been a possibility. Now they all climbed to nearly stratospheric heights in just a few seconds, the blast's shock wave chasing them up to 50,000 feet. Even with their welders' goggles down, none of the pilots was foolish enough to look back for fear they'd be blinded *and* turned into salt. Anyone within a hundred miles who'd been unlucky enough to look at the blast even for a second, though, was now permanently without sight. It was the most insidious weapon ever designed—by the evilest person who had ever lived.

Only when the strike force planes reached 55 Angels did they all level off and dare to look back. The flash was gone, and so was a lot of *Sekret Ostrov*.

Hunter clicked his chin mic again and this time uttered just two words: "Home Run."

The meaning was clear. The shipyard, the air base, and about two-thirds of the secret island had been vaporized. Most of the sawtooth mountain was gone. Most incredible, the previously frozen waters of the harbor were now boiling from the heat of the sun bomb's detonation.

Home Run.

The mission had been accomplished.

But had it been a success?

Had they been able to kill the devil himself?

As it turned out, they would not know right away—and that would make for a long journey home.

Chapter Two

Home Run.

The strike force's egress code had a double meaning.

Mission accomplished, yes.

But the UA pilots had already flown 4,000 miles—
and now they had to turn around and fly back home.

Leaving the secret island to burn in the wind and
snow, Hunter rolled his plane over, went down to 30,000
feet, and turned west. The rest of the strike force came
down with him and formed up on his tail.

Hunter's longtime friends, Ben Wa and JT Twomey,
were piloting the runway cratering jet, call sign Ringo 6.
They were also the flight leaders for the strike force, second in command to the Wingman.

Still flying through some heavy weather, they pulled
their Su-34 up off Hunter's wing. A quick radio check
brought some good news. All eight attack planes were
accounted for; everyone had survived the air strike.

The bad news was they hadn't gotten away un-
scathed.

Breaking out of the storm clouds, everyone was able
to get visuals on everyone else. It was not a pretty sight.
Almost all of the strike planes had taken shrapnel during

the 90-second raid. Some were leaking fluids; some were trailing smoke.

But when Hunter requested a flight check from each plane, it turned out shrapnel damage wasn't the main concern. It was the technical glitches. Just about everyone was having trouble with their flight systems. Nonsensical computer readouts, mysterious drains on prime electrical sources. Navigation lights blinking out, the cockpits heaters suddenly going cold.

Weird stuff.

None of this was unexpected. The United Americans had captured dozens of Su-34s during the recent Battle of New York. They now made up the bulk of the USA's resurrected air forces. But the UA had been flying the Su-34s in training for several weeks and had come to accept gremlins as almost always part of someone's flight. The problem was, when something went screwy during training it was a relatively short hop back to base.

At the moment, they were on the other side of the planet.

A twenty-hour, nearly 8,000-mile, polar-region air strike made for a long day. But if there was ever an aircraft that could do it, the Russian-designed Su-34VLR was it.

The big attack plane was sometimes called the Flying Winnebago. Officially an ultra-long-range strike fighter, its cockpit was considered roomy by modern standards. The two-man crew was able to walk around the bulbous cabin despite the presence of weapons systems and multiple panels for flight controls. There was a small galley, a small head, and enough room to lay out an air mattress, allowing one pilot to rest while the other watched over the plane's operations. Plus, the Su-34 could carry tons of exotic weapons and lots of fuel, so a far-flung air raid was exactly what it had been built for.

But the one thing the UA pilots feared even more than getting shot down was that after a trans-global deployment, dozens of daisy-chain aerial refuelings, one major aerial battle, and a bombing raid, the Russian airplanes would begin to break down, that their ruggedness would come up short.

And that's exactly what was happening.

Hunter would be the first to admit he'd fallen in love with the Su-34 at first touch. It felt good wrapped around him, plus he'd just lost his cherished F-16XL during the Battle of New York. But he'd come to realize his mad love for the foreign aircraft had been an infatuation, a crush—and it was dissipating quickly.

Even now, after checking on everyone else, he looked down at his own control panel to see it was lit up like a Christmas tree.

Of all the blinking lights, the one that was blinking most rapidly was big and red and in the center of his console. He didn't know much Russian, so he'd pasted labels over the entire control panel giving everything an English-language name. The big red flashing light was the main oil pressure warning gauge.

This was usually enough to make most pilots wet themselves. But Hunter just gave the light itself a flick of his finger and it stopped blinking.

No, he didn't know Russian, but he was getting a quick education on their airplanes. They all were.

He took the time to deal with the other warning lights in the same way. Give them a smack and they usually went out. If they didn't, smack them again. If they still stayed lit, then you might have a problem.

This time all of the warning lights on his console went out—except one.

It was the starboard engine exhaust-fail warning light. Just a slight vibration in the stick told Hunter this was actually an accurate reading. He pushed the plane ahead of the formation and violently pulled back on the controls, essentially causing the plane to hang in the air for a moment.

Then he pushed the nose over, hit the throttles again and did two twists to the right. The faulty air flap was jarred back into position and the exhaust-fail light blinked out.

For now.

The way Hunter flew, the way his friends flew—they *needed* advanced technology to do what they had to do. But they also needed a plane that could stay in one piece, at least to the end of the mission. Jet fighters that could be fixed with a hammer just weren't the American way.

That's why early in their training for the raid, some of the UA pilots had begun calling their planes "Fu-34s."

The squadron flew a ragged formation for the next half hour. But every minute seemed to bring a new drama.

One of the attack planes, Moondog 8, was being flown by two majors from the Football City Air Corps, Steve Ward and Henry Hudson. They were losing fuel not because of AA shrapnel but because a valve in their main fuel line was stuck open and leaking heavily.

At the same time, a damaged buddy tanker, Fab 4, flown by Hunter's friend, Rene Frost of the Free Canadian Air Force, and his co-pilot, Donny Marcotte, was having trouble because that very same fuel valve was stuck nearly shut.

But it was a radio message from Moondog 3 that changed everything.

This plane was being flown by Hunter's very good *amigo*, Captain Crunch, and his co-pilot, Elvis IV. Crunchy was a primo pilot—he'd run the famous Ace Wrecking Company in the early years after the Big War, hiring himself out as a two-ship mercenary bombing outfit. But he was a loyal American, and so was Elvis IV.

But now Crunch was in real trouble.

"I'm down to forty-nine universal and draining fast," he reported starkly.

No one wanted to hear this. Crunch's jet was literally in the process of a long crash. He was losing electrical power faster than his backup systems could keep providing auxiliary juice.

In the old days they called this a catastrophic flight failure in process. When the electrical power indicator got below 40, the airplane's fuel pumps would seize and the plane would go down.

Hunter took a quick look at his flight computer, calling up his moving map display. Like everything else Russian, it was grainy and unfocused. But he was able to tell they were somewhere over the northernmost edge of what used to be Scandinavia. Just a hundred miles beyond was the North Atlantic Ocean—sure death for anyone having to ditch in it.

"We're at four-seven universal," Crunch reported. "Four-six . . . four-five . . ."

Hunter searched his onboard computer mission page, whacking the screen twice to get it to cooperate. He called up the raid's emergency landing options and localized the search. But only one set of coordinates pinged back: a small island they'd dubbed Contingency Delta. It was forty miles south of them in an area that was now considered the far edge of the New Russian Empire.

Hunter called up an image of the island. It was oddly shaped, almost like a heart. Mountainous terrain, covered in snow, waves crashing on it from all sides. It looked abandoned and absolutely forbidding. But the intel said there was a runway down there somewhere.

As strike commander, he had to make a brutal decision.

"People with fuel and juice problems will set down on Contingency Delta," he announced. "I'll ride cover for them. Rest of strike, continue Home Run."

Then Hunter passed command of the attack force over to Ben and JT.

He would stay with the three stricken aircraft. The rest of the strike force would continue toward home, which in itself promised to be an adventure as it involved a dicey rendezvous with the newly christened USS *United States of America*, known to all as the USS *USA*.

The name wasn't meant to fool anybody. It was the old Russian behemoth aircraft carrier, *Admiral Isakov* painted U.S. Navy gray. Barely seaworthy after being the site of a massive battle just weeks before, the gigantic, battered flat top had been pressed into service as a recovery ship for the returning bombers.

It was waiting for them about halfway across the Atlantic, a postage stamp in the middle of a million square miles of dark, cold water. If they could find the ship and land on it, it would shave almost 1,000 miles off their journey. The other pilots had been hoping Hunter would lead them to the carrier; it just would have been easier that way.

But now that wasn't going to happen.

No one said anything to Hunter; no one tried to talk him out of it. Friends don't leave friends behind. Simple as that.

"We'll mark your location," Ben radioed him somberly. "Hang in there. Try comm once you're down."

Then on his command, the remaining planes of the strike force climbed back to 40,000 feet and disappeared into the Arctic murk.

Chapter Three

The four remaining airplanes formed a ragged chevron, descended to 1,000 feet, and turned toward the island known as Contingency Delta.

Hunter was out front, navigating half on instruments, half on instinct. The weather grew worse the farther they flew. Thick clouds, high winds, and vicious snow squalls even a quarter mile up.

Crunch's condition continued to degrade. He'd shut down all but his most crucial electrical gear, but his power kept draining. With each minute, he was getting closer to the fatal 40 percent mark.

He had about two more minutes of flying left when they reached the coordinates where the island should have been. But the cloud cover was so thick even their infrared scopes couldn't penetrate it.

Flying any lower in what might be a blind search would have been extremely dangerous, as they were sure there were lots of mountains down there, and in this weather, it would be very easy to plow into one. But when Crunch reported he was at 41-percent power, Hunter knew it was time for desperate measures.

So he closed his eyes and asked the cosmos for help. It took a few moments, but then he felt a jolt of electricity go through him. When he opened his eyes again, he saw a small hole had opened up in the cloud cover just off his plane's left wing. Directly below it was the heart-shaped island.

He had no time to question how it happened. He immediately peeled off from the others and went down to just 100 feet. According to Contingency Delta, the island's runway was on a cliff hanging out over its western coast. Still, it was only because the ocean wind was blowing so fiercely that he was able to spot the airstrip. Huge snowdrifts covered one end of it, but thanks to the high gale, some of the hard surface was partially cleared and visible.

Hunter reported this back to the other three planes and then went in first. Wheels down, nose up, he hoped the flare from his exhaust nozzles would melt some of the snow fouling the landing strip. He hit the runway at 120 knots and quickly reversed his engines, but his plane seemed to roll forever, a blizzard of slushy ice covering his canopy, knocking his visibility down to zero.

He held the control stick straight and tight and finally came to an abrupt, noisy halt, whacking his head hard against the control panel. Even with his helmet on, he felt like he'd been hit with a sledgehammer.

Crunch came down right behind him. He hit the runway hard as well, his big plane first skidding left then, thanks to the overcompensating automatic controls, sliding mightily to the right. It fishtailed like this for more than a half mile until finally its nose smashed into a massive snowbank on the side of the runway. It was like hitting a wall. The landing was so violent it blew out all of the plane's tires and collapsed its landing gear.

Hunter scrambled out of his plane and rushed over to the Crunchy's jet. It was already engulfed in thick yellow smoke, and flames were erupting under its fuel tanks. Climbing up on its duck-billed nose, he used the butt of his .357 Magnum pistol to break the glass of the plane's forward canopy. He looked in to find Crunch and Elvis IV still strapped in their seats, both unconscious.

A loud sizzling noise told him the plane was just seconds away from blowing up. This was not good. Access to the Su-34 was from the bottom, through a door behind the landing gear. At the moment, it was glaring just how bad a design that was.

He began kicking the canopy panel with the hole in it, and thank God, true to form, the Russian-made glass broke away somewhat easily. He crawled into the cockpit even as the sizzling noise was getting louder. He pulled Elvis out first, cutting away his seat belts, pushing his limp body through the hole in the glass and dropping him to the snow below.

Freeing Crunch was more difficult. His seat was severely mangled and dangerously close to ejecting itself, taking them both with it. Hunter began cutting away at his friend's safety harness as quickly and carefully as he could. The sizzling got even louder, the smoke more intense and choking. The restraints finally gave way, though, and Hunter pulled his friend out.

Elvis was conscious again; landing head first in the snow bank had brought him to. Still groggy, he helped Hunter carry Crunch down and away from the burning airplane.

They'd made it about twenty feet before the Russian jet blew up. The blast threw all three of them into a snow drift, a rain of fiery debris coming down on top of them, melting everything to a greasy sludge. This lasted for a few long seconds before it got quiet again.

When they emerged from the dirty snow, they saw the back half of Moondog 3 was little more than a burning, charred skeleton with ash and cinders caught in a whirlwind above it. The explosion had been that intense.

Hunter threw more snow in Crunch's face and his colleague finally came to with a cough.

"Where the fuck are we?" he moaned, shaking his aching head.

But his words were drowned out by another thunderous roar going over them.

It was Fab 4, the damaged buddy tanker piloted by Frost and Marcotte. Hop-scotching Crunch's burning wreck, the pilots mimicked his approach, pulling their nose up to drain off airspeed before coming down.

The result was nearly the same, though. It was a very hard landing. No sooner had it come to a halt when a stream of hot vapor began pouring out of the engines, engulfing the plane in another sick, yellow fog. Perfect conditions to start a catastrophic fire.

Battered though they were, Hunter, Crunch, and Elvis rushed to the plane and began desperately throwing snow onto its exhaust nozzles, trying to cool them off. Climbing down from the cockpit, Frost and Marcotte joined them. Then together, and with supreme effort, the five of them pushed the stricken fighter ten feet to one side.

That's when the last plane—Moondog 8, piloted by the Football City pilots Ward and Hudson—came barreling in. It was battling tremendously high winds, and about five seconds before touching down, was hit by a vicious downdraft.

The plane's left landing gear bent on contact with the runway, causing the left wing to hit the pavement, violently spinning the plane.

But Ward kept his cool and buried his right-engine throttle. A small explosion of flame and smoke came out of its nozzle, but miraculously the maneuver stopped the gyration and the airplane came to a smoky stop.

Then, suddenly, it was over.

They looked around. The wind was blowing fiercely; the snow felt like little ice cubes hitting them. It was Scandinavia at noontime, dark, dank, and frigid. There was nothing but a high, jagged, snowy mountain to the east. To the west, just a few hundred feet away, was the edge of the cliff. At its bottom was a very rocky shoreline with massive waves breaking on it.

Beyond that was the cold, gray, stormy North Atlantic.

More revived now, Crunch repeated his line, with more emphasis this time: "Where *the fuck* are we?"

Hunter shook his head and groaned.

"Exactly," he said.

Chapter Four

After covering their airplanes as best they could in snow, the seven pilots retreated to Hunter's Su-34 and stuffed themselves inside.

It proved a tight fit even in the expansive cockpit. But his plane was the most intact of the four, and its power systems still worked, and that meant heat. The cabin amenities designed for two on what the Russians had envisioned as ultra-long strike missions would, at the moment, provide warmth and shelter for the American pilots, shielding them from the wild Scandinavian weather outside.

They'd liberated several boxes of MRE rations from their damaged jets. Water was not a problem; they just reached outside and grabbed a fistful of snow. Five minutes later it was boiling in a pot for instant coffee.

But the mood was definitely gloomy. They ate a meal of soggy, lukewarm MREs in near silence. Out in the middle of nowhere didn't even come close to describing their situation. They were stranded on a heart-shaped chunk of ice next to the raging North Atlantic with only one working aircraft that at most could lift off with five people on board.

Several times during and then after the glum meal, they took turns trying to contact Ben and JT, knowing distance and location were both working against them. But after dozens of attempts, they finally gave up.

Exhausted and dejected, they haphazardly laid out some air mattresses and survival blankets on the cockpit floor and went to sleep.

All except Hunter.

Hours passed.

When the other pilots woke up, they found the Wingman out in a storm, fighting the high winds and blowing snow, salvaging parts from the disabled attack planes. Meanwhile, the snow had been coming down so steadily it had practically hidden all four stranded aircraft.

They beckoned him in and, somewhat reluctantly, he agreed.

He accepted a cup of Nescafe and then announced: "OK—this is how we get out of this mess."

It took him under a minute to explain. By cannibalizing workable parts from Moondog 8, and a few crucial ones from his own plane, they could put them into the Frost's buddy tanker, solve his fuel valve problem, and make it flyable again. Then they could drain all the fuel from Ward's plane, and some from his own, and put it into the tanker's two large external pods, almost filling both of them.

That would give them not just one good airplane, but one that was a buddy tanker which, with a few minor adjustments, could literally refuel itself in flight.

The pilots considered the wild idea. With any aircraft it was always a question of weight versus fuel. The less weight you have, the less fuel you will burn. The more fuel you have on board, the farther you will go.

Hunter was just adding them altogether.

But Crunch shook his head. He'd done the calculations as well. Distance divided by fuel. Fuel divided by weight. It worked out only if the maximum number of people aboard the Phoenix airplane was six. The plan was that close to the margins.

"We're not leaving you here," he told Hunter directly.

But Hunter just waved his concerns away.

"It's the only solution that makes sense," Hunter told him. "And if it works, you guys will get off this ice cube."

Crunch was still shaking his head, though. "But if you take parts and fuel from your plane to do it, you could be stranding yourself here for a very long time—maybe forever."

Hunter shrugged. "You know where I am. Just come back with a good buddy tanker and drop me a couple new ITEG interfaces. I put them in and I'll get off here, too. We'll all be home by the end of the week."

But now Frost spoke up.

"Even if we can take off with so many people on board, Hawk," he said. "You know the Su-34 isn't exactly designed to be fuel efficient; that's why it carries so much fuel. With all of us crammed inside, weighing it down, we could still run out of gas long before we get to the carrier."

"Not if you do two things," Hunter said. "First, turn off one of your engines once you get up there."

The pilots all gasped—but it made sense. The Su-34 *could* limp along on just one engine. It would make for a longer, bumpier ride and some monumental steering and lording over the controls. But it could be done.

"Number two," Hunter went on. "Once you're airborne, try like crazy to get in touch with the carrier. Because I'm thinking that in the three extra days we'll lose being out here, they'll be steaming full-out in this direction, based on the info the rest of the strike force gave them. If you can contact them quickly and get a vector, I'm sure it will cut down on the distance you'll have to fly to reach it."

But Crunch remained solidly opposed to the scheme.

"I think a better idea is you come with us and we risk the fuel situation," he said.

Hunter just smiled at his old friend. "Do you really want me to order you to do this?"

A minute went by in complete silence. Finally, the six other pilots just looked at each other and then back at him, grim acceptance on their faces. As he was famous for, Hunter had distilled the complicating factors down to a detailed plan and made it as simple as possible.

True, there were a lot of "ifs." But one thing they all agreed on: when it came to getting out of tight situations, Hunter always seemed to be right.

Chapter Five

The next twenty-four hours proved long, cold, and strenuous.

They were so far north the sun barely made it above the horizon, and then only for a few hours. They had small trouble lights with them, and Hunter's nose beacon still worked, so they weren't stuck in complete darkness. But the wind and snow were relentless.

Still they worked out a system. Hunter and Crunch did the installations; the others cannibalized the needed parts from Ward's and Hudson's aircraft and even a few from Hunter's plane.

It was endless, backbreaking, uncomfortable work. But by the morning of the third day, Frost's reworked Fab 4 buddy tanker was ready to take off.

Or at least try to.

They all knew it was going to be a close-run thing. The winds sweeping across the cliffside runway would provide plenty of lift. That wouldn't be a problem.

The problem was power. The Su-34 was a large air-plane for a fighter-bomber; it was designed that way. And at this point, Fab 4 was no longer carrying any ord-nance, which helped weight-wise. Also, once its large external fuel tanks were emptied, they could be jettisoned, further lightening its load.

But none of that could happen unless it was airborne. Getting off the ground would be the biggest challenge.

Once ready, the pilots crowded into the tanker's cockpit. Because their extra weight would affect the plane's center of gravity, they laid down on the cabin's deck to spread out the load.

Frost would pilot and Crunch would be in the co-pilot's seat for the takeoff. They were the most experienced fliers. If the plane got airborne, they could rotate people at the controls until they reached the aircraft carrier . . . or went into the sea.

Either way, they had at least an eight-hour flight ahead of them.

Hunter made one final check of the buddy tanker's flight systems. Then he shook hands with everyone. In turn, each promised he would personally make sure he got off the icy rock.

"Just make sure you bring more than one airplane," he told them.

Then he was gone, climbing down out of the cockpit and making sure the bottom hatch was secured.

He did his best at hand signaling Frost to turn this way and that, positioning the plane so it was facing into the brutal wind.

Then he crossed his fingers—behind his back, of course—just praying both of the jet's engines would start. They coughed a couple of times, but finally lit and went up to full power. There was no time for celebration. Because of the fuel situation, they couldn't waste a second more on the ground.

Frost and Crunch gave Hunter a thumbs-up and a salute. Then Frost hit the throttles.

The plane immediately began moving, roaring down the bumpy runway with a great burst of fire and wet exhaust. A typical takeoff roll for an Su-34 was about 2,000 feet. Frost lifted off in half that, using the fierce winds to wrest the big, overloaded fighter off the snowy, slippery ground.

He pulled up the landing gear and steered hard to starboard so he was out over the cliff clean, technically in flight. But the plane hung in the air for a few long seconds, teetering between being airborne and going into the Atlantic.

It took longer than it should have, but finally the physics kicked in and the big jet started moving forward.

Frost immediately put it on its tail and flew up toward 20,000 feet. That's when they planned to level off, turn off one of the engines and then settle in for a long, cold ride to somewhere—or nowhere.

Hunter was able to keep the flare of the plane's engines in sight for almost a half-minute before he finally lost it in the thick storm clouds. It took another couple of minutes for the noise to disappear. At the end of it, he could have sworn he heard Frost shut down one engine, but it might have been just his imagination.

In any case, once the noise had faded for good and the storm clouds closed back in, he knew he was alone for sure.

The next six hours moved slowly.

Hunter did his best to keep busy working on his airplane's electronics, rewiring and bypassing some redundant systems, the key components of which they'd installed in the Fab 4.

Still, it was tough to keep his mind on what needed to be done.

He'd been in tough spots before.

But nothing like this.

Then, just when he thought it couldn't get worse—it did.

This new hell came via his cockpit radio. It suddenly burst to life and, seconds later, he was talking to his friend, Mike Fitzgerald.

Fitz was calling from his submarine, still up in the Kara Sea off Siberia. After hours trying to locate Hunter, he'd finally gotten through—but the connection was extremely weak.

Hunter quickly told him the story about the mass crash-landing on the windblown island, and how the others had managed to get off earlier that day.

Then Fitz got to the heart of the matter.

"Three words, Hawk," he told Hunter gravely. "We missed him."

Fitz explained: His propeller-driven recon drone had captured the entire raid on video and sent it back to the sub before being obliterated in the sun bomb blast. But while the destruction was widespread, the camera showed Viktor's sub disappearing just seconds before the nuke went off. He said it was hard to explain how. One moment the submarine could be clearly seen docked at the shipyard's center block pier—in the next moment it is gone, disappearing in the strange red smoke. This was not an embarkation; the sub didn't suddenly put to sea and run. In fact, this would have been impossible, because a submarine would have to ride on the surface until getting out of the shipyard's relatively shallow harbor, a distance of at least a half mile—where Fitz's own super-sub had been waiting for it.

The truth was, Viktor's sub had simply vanished into the crimson smoke.

Their radio connection started to break up. Fitz told Hunter he would contact the USS *USA* and ascertain the fate of their friends aboard the Fab 4 as well as the rest of the strike force.

Then the communication suddenly ended and Fitz was gone. Hunter tried for thirty minutes to get him back, but with no luck

At that point, he just slumped into his pilot's seat and closed his eyes.

We . . . missed . . . him.

These words now started bouncing around his head and would not stop.

Viktor Robotov . . .

"Damn," Hunter whispered. "He *is* the devil."

Chapter Six

Hunter worked nonstop for the entire next day.

Most of it was spent in the wind, cold, and sleet, trying to fish out the last workable components from Ward's plane needed for his own jet to get airborne again.

He had few tools and no means of lifting anything heavy, so it involved a lot of crawling through the dark, disabled aircraft, hoping that whatever parts he could salvage were still useable.

He finally lay down to rest on the twenty-fifth hour. Bruised, battered, and dirty, he could sleep only in fits. There was too much on his mind. One big concern was running out of fuel needed to turn his engines on for five minutes every six hours to run the generators that charged the batteries that powered the cockpit heaters. He was also sick of eating MREs, the instant coffee was gone, and the bump on his head was giving him one long headache.

But nothing was bothering him more than the devastating news from Fitz. All the planning, all the preparations, the logistics of flying a trans-global air strike, the time, the energy, and effort a couple of hundred people had put in, to finally whack Viktor—and for what?

The bastard still got away.

He woke up the next day, feeling more exhausted than ever.

His back hurt; his head hurt. His hands were chapped and bloody. He had charred metal filings stuck to his neck and ears and could taste them in his mouth. He was miserable, helmet to boots.

He needed a break.

So he decided to climb the nearby mountain.

He cleaned himself up, packed a little food, a couple of survival blankets, his night vision goggles, and his .357 Magnum and set out. He guessed it would take him ten hours to make the 1,500-foot ascent. Just like on *Sekret Ostrov*, the mountain was sawtoothed and steep. But just an hour into his journey and very unexpectedly, he found an ancient pathway that cut through many of the jagged outcrops and led directly to the summit. It was still a workout, though, especially in the wind and blowing snow.

But there was a method to his madness. As miserable as the place was, Contingency Delta had been a lifesaver for them. But all it was to him was a point on a crude electronic map of northwest Scandinavia. With each step up the mountain, he tried to convince himself that if he knew exactly where he was, if he knew just how far he was from home, it would somehow make him feel better.

From what he could tell, at ground level the heart-shaped island was almost always covered with sea fog and low-hanging clouds. But the higher he climbed, the more the mist cleared and, thanks to his night vision goggles, the more of the island he could see. He discovered the place had some surprising features.

First, there was no permafrost along its coastline, nor any ice layer above the tide mark. This was the near-Arctic. There should have been a ring of sea ice surrounding the island. But there wasn't.

Even stranger was the vegetation. It was everywhere on the side of the mountain, mostly growing between the sharply jagged rocks. But he could also see flora along the coastline below the cliffs. Some of it looked almost tropical.

And there was no seaweed—anywhere.

He knew there was only one explanation. The island must be somewhere near the end of the warm-water Gulfstream.

He reached the mountain's peak a couple of hours earlier than anticipated. Wrapping himself in the two survival blankets, he ate a stale MRE biscuit in celebration.

Then he watched the sun slip below the western horizon, ending its brief stay.

Night fell, but it took another half hour before the clouds overhead finally blew away and he could see the stars. He counted the brightest ones and did some quick calculations. His conclusion? If his math was right, Contingency Delta was actually one of the Weather Islands, located off the western coast of what used to be Sweden.

"But if this is Sweden," he wondered aloud, "where are all the blondes?"

Having gotten what he came for, he knew it was time to prepare for his descent. But he couldn't help staying for a few more minutes, remaining immobile and unable to look anywhere but to the west. He stared off in that direction for so long he started to imagine he could see the lights of the East Coast twinkling just over the horizon. He so mightily wished he was there. He missed America, he missed his girlfriend, Sara, and he missed his old F-16XL—all in so many ways.

He fell to his knees, head in his hands. He was seriously bummed out, not the usual state of affairs for him. No matter how dire the situation, he almost always found some ray of hope, something to grasp onto.

But not this time.

At least not yet.

*****

It was about 10 p.m. when he finally got ready for the long climb down.

He couldn't imagine anything waiting for him below besides more miserable weather and the endless search for the workable parts he needed to get off the frigid heart-shaped island.

He folded up the survival blankets and strapped them to his back. Then he put away his night vision goggles, picked up his .357 Magnum and turned to go.

That's when a glint of light caught his eye.

It came out of the mist north of him. Maybe a quarter-mile away and a thousand feet down, tucked inside the largest crevice on this side of the mountain and facing the roaring Atlantic, he could see two long, winding rows of amber lights.

"Jessuz," he breathed. "No freaking way."

He hastily put his night vision goggles back on and turned them up to high. In that moment, a gust of wind blew away the clouds of fog and he found himself looking down at a tiny village.

A few dozen small houses, narrow streets winding through them, all lit by dual rows of gaslights.

He couldn't believe it.

People actually *lived* here . . .

He instinctively took his .357 back out.

Were they Russians?

That was his first thought—a Russian outpost. But just as quickly, something told him no.

This was not a military installation. Nor were they sea shacks—plus there were no boats about. Instead, it was a collection of picturesque, if slightly weather-beaten cottages. Nothing about them was built at a right angle, and from what he could see, every one of them had some kind of ornamentation attached to it—colorful roofs and shutters, gas lamps on the doors, candles in the windows.

He turned the NVG telescoping feature on and got a slightly closer look. Just about every house had something else: a small garden jammed into a minuscule front lawn. And many of these gardens were cluttered with statues of gnomes.

"British?" he thought. "Way up here?'

Chapter Seven

It was an hour before midnight by the time he reached the outskirts of the small village.

While his climb up had been just this side of self-torture, he seemed to glide back down the mountain. The entire descent took on a strange, dreamy quality; he didn't feel cold or isolated or tired anymore. Aided greatly by his night vision goggles, he managed to keep the tiny settlement in sight throughout the journey down, just praying the place wouldn't suddenly disappear.

He paused at a small ice bridge that led over one last crevice and into the village itself. The main street was deserted and the place was deathly quiet. He retrieved his .357 Magnum from his boot holster again, but also took out the small American flag he always carried in his breast pocket. Should there be a language barrier here, the flag would quickly identify where he was from.

He slowly walked across the ice bridge into town, trying to stay in the shadows. Nothing he could see indicated any Russians were about. Just the opposite. From ground level, the village looked even more like a British version of a Scandinavian Christmas card. The houses were painted in reds, blues, and yellows; the shop signs featured Old English-style lettering. It seemed every other doorway led to a confectionary shop, and he counted three fish-and-chips restaurants just within one block. It was like a little piece of the Big Crumpet broke off and floated up here.

All the houses and shops were locked up tight—except one. At the end of the street, lights ablaze, was the town tavern.

He stole up to the building, peeked in a side window and saw a smoky, crowded bar with about fifty people drinking and another dozen dancing. A priceless Wurlitzer jukebox provided the tunes. It looked rowdy but civilized.

These people were definitely not Russian. They didn't even seem Scandinavian. For want of a better word, they seemed *happy*.

Drunk, but happy.

Now what?

He was stranded here, on a tiny, heart-shaped, North Atlantic snowball that, until just a short while ago, he would have sworn was uninhabitable. Should he blow his cover and make contact?

That question was answered for him a moment later in a way so unusual, he would remember it to his dying day.

The door next to him suddenly opened and a girl in her late twenties stepped out. She had curly, strawberry blonde hair, was dressed in a plaid shirt and jeans, and had an apron on. She was also wearing a white baseball cap.

She looked at him as if they already knew each other.

"Well, are you coming in?" she asked him.

But Hunter couldn't move. Feeling like he'd been hit by another kind of sledgehammer, he was frozen just looking at her.

She was so beautiful . . .

"It's very cold out," she added, almost scolding him. "Come on, get in here."

Hunter finally got his feet moving and stepped into the tavern.

But as soon as he came through the door, everything inside stopped.

A gasp went through the crowd. Several females cried out.

Then one voice shouted: "Oh my God —it's Hawk Hunter!"

Chapter Eight

He was mobbed at the door.

Everyone in the place wanted to hug him, kiss him—men, women, even a few kids.

He knew he was known around the postwar world; that's just the way it was.

But way up here? In the middle of nowhere?

The crowd dragged him to a table just off the bar, the best seat in the house. He was quickly surrounded, with about a dozen people crowding in very close to him. He was a rock star to them. Many even reached out to touch his hair.

They began firing questions at him in English, all the same version of: What are you doing here?

He tried to explain via the short version: He'd been forced to crash land on the other side of the island and his colleagues were coming back for him soon. But the patrons really didn't care. They didn't get many visitors, and here was a real-life celebrity.

Just as it got to the point of almost overwhelming, an older man slid into the seat next to him, shooing many of the patrons away. He was wearing the green camo combat uniform of the European Free Forces, a mercenary group that had fought the Russians valiantly, though in vain, during World War III.

He introduced himself as Ross Sharp, better known as the Major. He was ex-SAS, but lost his right leg during the Falklands War. Still he fought with EFF on the Continent and was proud of his service. He boozily told Hunter that he would be honored to serve as his guide for as long as he was on the island.

A huge bowl of oyster stew arrived at the table along with more than a dozen glasses of beer. Hunter couldn't help it. He dug in.

As he ate and drank, Sharp explained the townspeople were, in fact, Euro-Survivors—people in Europe who'd lived through World War III and decided to go elsewhere after the brief but catastrophic hostilities.

Leaving England, they traveled north, away from the poison gas, the radioactivity, and the horror of impending Russian occupation and recreated a quaint Victorian village on this then-uninhabited Swedish island, a place that was indeed near the terminus of the Gulf Stream. It was also close to the best oyster fishing in the world. In fact, the primary food source here was . . . oysters.

According to the Major, that led to a very unusual situation.

"Look around this room," he told Hunter as yet another round of beers arrived. "What do you see?"

Hunter shrugged. "Inebriation?"

"Inebriated females," the Major corrected him.

Hunter did a more thorough scan of the bar; Sharp was right. Of the sixty or so people on hand, more than two-thirds were women, most in their twenties, thirties, or early forties. Some were dressed as men, and that had slowed the counting process. But there was no doubt males were in the minority here.

"But that's a good thing!" the Major told him, reading his mind.

He explained most of the island's residents were females because most of the men never returned from World War III, now more than ten years ago.

But because most of the population was female, the few males—however old they might be—were in the Swedish phrase: *mycket lycklig bortom anledning.*

Lucky beyond all reason.

That's where all the oysters came in handy.

Hunter drained three bowls of stew and shotgunned a half-dozen beers in about forty-five minutes. Meanwhile, the Major called two or three people at a time over to the table, doing brief but polite introductions until the Wingman had met everybody. Lots of Smiths, Taylors, and Morgans. Lots of Sophies, Charlottes, and Poppys. The women patrons were especially friendly.

Buzzed and getting full, Hunter couldn't believe he'd fallen into such a lucky situation. The hospitality was off the charts and out of the blue. This cold, harsh place had almost instantly turned warm and inviting.

Plus, they had beer.

But then the clock struck midnight and everything changed. The bar suddenly shut down, the jukebox plug was pulled. All conversation ceased.

The Major nudged him in the ribs.

"Time to go, mate," he said, draining the last of his beer.

Hunter was confused. People were leaving the bar in a hasty, but almost routine fashion.

"Go where?" he asked the old soldier. "Home?"

Sharp shook his head.

"No, my boy," he said, sliding out of his seat. "It's time to go to the cellars."

The next thing Hunter knew, he and the Major were stumbling out of the pub, and along with the rest of the patrons, hurried across the street to a set of stairs that led underground.

Down they went, and at first Hunter thought he was in a wine cellar. But then he saw mattresses and blankets and candles and teapots steaming over lit Sterno cans. Besides the bar patrons, about another hundred people were already here, mostly women and children. Some of the kids were scared.

Only then did it dawn on him.

He was in an air raid shelter.

The bombs started dropping a few seconds later.

Even locked in a chamber twenty feet below ground, Hunter guessed they were cluster munitions, canisters designed to release dozens of small bomblets capable of doing some quick and brutal damage.

Hunter was drunk-ish—and there was an air of unreality all around him. But it was not entirely due to the strong lager.

"Who is bombing you?" he asked the Major.

"The Russians, who else?" was the reply.

He was so matter of fact it gave Hunter pause.

"But how did you know they were coming?"

The Major took a flask out of his pocket. "Every Saturday night at midnight they fly over and drop bombs on us. We have to close the pub for a while due to putting out the fires and the clean-up and such. But then everything goes back to normal."

Hunter's head was spinning now.

"But . . . *why* are they doing this?" he asked, uncharacteristically turning down an offer for a swig of the flask.

So the Major took one for him.

"There's a piss-poor Russian air base on the next island over," he explained. "A half-dozen old airplanes, maybe twenty Reds in all. No other Russians for hundreds of miles around. Well, we live better over here than they do over there—and they're jealous of that. They wanted to be able to come over here and drink our beer and get with our women, but no one here wanted any part of it.

"So, to show their displeasure, every Saturday at midnight, they bomb us with glorified firecrackers. And depending how drunk they are, they'll be back a couple times at least. And then we get a radio message from them that always says the same thing: *Kak zhe dostala eta voyna! Esli b ne ona, my b seychas gde-nibud zazhigali.*"

Hunter could only shrug. He didn't know much Russian, so the Major did a rough translation: "We are sick of this little war. We could all be partying right now."

Sharp's distaste was obvious. "And we already know what kind of party they would like to have. We call it 'The Nonsense.' But I'm afraid someday they'll get sober and figure out how to mount an invasion and come over in force."

"And you have no defense against them?" Hunter asked.

"Not really," Sharp confessed. "We have an airplane, but no one to fly it, and . . ."

Hunter gently interrupted him. "You have an airplane here?"

The Major took another swig from his flask. "Yes, over at the airport," he replied.

"The airport?"

"It's just over the next hill," the Major said. "Isn't that where you were forced to land?"

"Yes," Hunter told him. "But I didn't see any airport, just a runway and barely that."

Sharp managed a weak smile. "Maybe you just weren't looking in the right place," he said.

Hunter heard him, but he was already on to the next thing. He was unlocking the door to the shelter, and to the horror of the people inside, climbed out.

He reached the street just in time to see the pair of Russian planes pull a wide turn over the town, heading back to their base.

Just as he suspected, they were Su-25 Frogfoots, ground attack airplanes that were similar but sub-par to America's more famous A-10 Thunderbolt II. And judging by the remains of what had been dropped on the small town, he was certain now they'd been cluster bombs.

But what was happening didn't make sense. Bombing this little village was surreal enough, but cluster bombs were designed to be used against troops in battle. Dropping them on any kind of hardened target was odd. They'd plastered the small village with shrapnel and a few small fires were blazing away, but there was surprisingly little damage. Just enough to make the whole thing miserable—and that was the point, he supposed.

His anger got the best of him. He took out the .357 Magnum and fired six rounds at the retreating airplanes, but to no effect.

The Major had climbed out after him by this time and tried to pull him back into the shelter. But Hunter had other ideas.

"Do you have any all-terrain vehicles here?" he asked the veteran officer.

"Would a Range Rover do?"

"You bet," Hunter said. "Can you get me back to the airport—and show me where your airplane is?"

"I can—if you don't mind driving with someone under the influence."

Hunter put his flight helmet back on.

"Don't worry," he told Sharp. "It won't be the first time."

Chapter Nine

They were at the runway twenty minutes later, the road around the bottom of the mountain was a much easier and quicker route than climbing over the thing.

On arrival, Hunter saw only what he'd left: his Su-34 and the two other disabled planes buried in snow. He could barely see the wind-swept airstrip, never mind an airport.

But it was there.

The Major simply directed his attention to a spot hard up against the mountainside, not 500 yards from where his Su-34 was parked.

Sure enough, there was a hangar and a small control tower there.

Built low to the ground, they were not simply painted snow white; they were camouflaged with *gradients* of white paint, to blend in perfectly with the surroundings. The dull shadows of the Scandinavian night only aided the charade.

"Freaking Swedes," Hunter said in admiration. "They were the smartest cats in the world when it came to hiding in the snow. I've been here for three days and never saw it."

But now he understood why this place—Contingency Delta—showed up on his flight map. Though Sweden was traditionally out on its own politically, behind the scenes Hunter knew their military always worked in close cooperation with the West, especially the United States. This place might have even been used by American planes in the past.

"They were indeed masters of their environment," the Major said. "It's a pity because so many were displaced, there aren't many left up around this part of the world."

They drove over to the pair of buildings; even up close they were hard to pick out.

When they finally reached the hangar, Hunter stepped out of the Range Rover and put his hand on the air barn's door, just to see if it was real.

"This place is our one and only top secret," the Major told him. "Thank God for all this snow. Can you imagine if the Reds really started looking and found out they could actually land here?"

He opened the hangar's lock and pushed the doors aside. "Hope you haven't had enough surprises for one day," he said over his shoulder.

Hunter had a small pen flashlight, but it was enough illumination to see the aircraft in front of them. But like everything else on the island, there was an air of unreality around it.

It was a SAAB-21 propeller-driven attack plane . . . from the early 1950s. Twin boom, pusher propeller. It looked like a distant, smaller, hipper cousin to the legendary P-38 Lightning.

But it was an odd duck. And an antique.

Hunter walked around the plane, giving it a quick situational check. Like a lot of Swedish technology, it was part machine, part piece of art. But this creation had a definite bite in the form of a 50-mm cannon sticking out of its nose. It was even loaded.

"We come up and start the engine every few weeks," the Major explained. "We fire the gun twice a year. It's more of a ritual, I suppose. But again, none of us knows how to fly."

Hunter completed his trip around the aircraft.

"That's OK," he said. "Because I do."

Chapter Ten

The two Russian Frogfoots flew back to their base, refueled—and rearmed.

These were the standing orders from their commander. If it was Saturday night, then bomb the next island over at least twice. If the fuel allotment allowed, a third flight could be added. The two Frogfoot pilots, part of a squadron of six, would rather have been sleeping. But for this night, they'd drawn the short straws.

Their base, known simply as K-2, was the very edge of the expansive New Russian Empire. A half-dozen old planes, a potholed runway, a decrepit hangar and barracks, neither with very much heat. It was as isolated a frontier post as one could get. No one wanted to be here.

But at least the missions were brief. A short, two-mile flight over to the heart-shaped island, spot the lights of the small town, drop weapons, fly home. It took less than ten minutes from beginning to end.

On returning, the two Russian pilots drank some hot tea and vodka, then climbed back into their airplanes. Takeoff was normal; within a minute they were once again approaching the neighboring island just two miles across an icy strait. They began a long sweep south that would put them over the village at about 500 feet. Each plane was carrying two GBU cluster bombs on its wings. The thinking was this routine run would be a carbon copy of their earlier flight.

But it didn't go that way.

Three quarters into their turn south, the pilots were stunned when their rudimentary air-defense radars showed another aircraft was up here with them. It was just a blip on their screens, flying somewhere above them, coming from the north. The two pilots had been at K-2 for more than a year, and nothing like this had happened before. The only airplanes flying way up here wore Russian markings.

Until now.

The sudden appearance of the intruder caused the Frogfoot pilots to abort their bombing run, pull up, and turn out over the sea. The Russian aircraft were attack planes. They dropped bombs. They weren't designed to dogfight.

And while each carried a GP 30-caliber detachable gun pod, this weapon was meant to shoot at targets on the ground. It was of little use in air-to-air combat. Bad news for the Russian flyers.

As soon as both Frogfoots had cleared the island and were speeding low over the dark, stormy ocean, the intruder pounced.

Unlike the Russian planes, this aircraft was sporting a cannon. In a dogfight, the ultimate winner might need up to one hundred machine gun rounds to down his opponent. But just one well-placed cannon shot could critically damage an aircraft; several hits and it was most likely doomed.

The mystery plane came straight down at them, out of the night, its massive gun exploding with a stream of shells, every fifth one being a luminous tracer round.

It was all over almost as soon as it happened. The attacker's triangulation and aim were so precise, both Frogfoot pilots suddenly found themselves with perforated tail sections. The cannon fire had hit them five times each in just one ten-round burst.

Both pilots now desperately turned back toward the island. Their planes were mortally wounded and both had to bail out. But they wanted to be over land—any land—before they pulled the ejection handle.

Just as they completed this desperate maneuver, their mystery assailant flew by them. Even in their perilous state, the two pilots were astonished to see the victor of their brief, one-sided encounter was a near-ancient, prop-driven SAAB-21, a plane built closer to the World War II era than now.

It didn't seem real to the pilots that a much slower, much older aircraft had bested them. Yet the flames pouring out of their tail sections told a different story.

Finally reaching land, they jettisoned their cluster bombs, struggled to get up to 1,000 feet, and finally punched out.

The Russian pilots parachuted onto the rocky beach not a quarter mile from the village, their dying airplanes crashing into the jagged mountain that divided the island in two.

Armed men and women were waiting for them as they floated down. They were immediately placed in custody.

As they were being led away, the old SAAB airplane flew overhead again, doing a perfect victory roll before disappearing back into the night.

Chapter Eleven

Just an hour later, the two Russians were sitting in the back seat of the Major's Range Rover bouncing along a very bumpy, snow-covered road heading east.

Hands bound by rope, hoods over their heads, they were taking the punishment of every twist and turn. The Rover and one behind it were heading to the other side of the heart-shaped island.

Not a word was spoken in all that time, which alarmed the Russians greatly. The people who put the hoods over their heads were all carrying shotguns. Few things ended peacefully in this part of the world when shotguns were involved.

It took about a half hour to reach what the islanders called Far Beach. The Range Rovers stopped at the edge of a small bay. The wind was howling and snow was blowing everywhere. The pilots were hustled out and made to kneel on a sandy mound looking out on the water.

Two miles away, across a dark strait, were the dim lights of the Russian K-2 air base. Finally, the pilots' hoods were pulled off and they realized where they were.

Then one man came up very close to them. He was wearing a pilot's suit and a pearl-white crash helmet with a lightning bolt on each side.

He was holding not a shotgun, but a massive .357 Magnum.

"Do you guys know who I am?" he asked them in English.

One pilot immediately shook his head no. But the other took a closer look—and then his face fell.

"Wingmanski?" he blurted out.

"Yes," Hunter said, keeping a straight face. That was a new one. "I'm Wingmanski . . . and I want you to take a message from me to your commander. Understand?"

Both pilots nodded enthusiastically.

"This crap on Saturday nights stops right now," he told them. "The women over here aren't interested. The people aren't interested. Simple as that. Tell him that and tell him I'm the one saying it."

But now the Russians were wondering how they were expected to get back to their island.

The Major answered their question by throwing a life raft in front of them. It began to noisily inflate as soon as it hit the ground.

The Russians looked at the small two-man float, then the hazardous waters of the strait and then back up at Hunter, horror coming across their faces.

But they didn't even have to ask the question.

Hunter just nodded.

"It's either this," he said, "or you can swim . . ."

A few minutes later, the bedraggled pilots embarked on their journey.

Using driftwood for paddles, they went around in circles a few times before finally pointing the raft in the right direction. Within two minutes they were out of sight.

The Major, Hunter, and the other armed villagers watched them go.

"Really? Simple as that?" the Major wondered aloud.

Hunter shook his head.

"I wish," he replied. "But knowing the Russians, it's not over. And they're probably not going to wait until next Saturday night."

Chapter Twelve

The weak sun came and went, the gloom gathered over the heart-shaped island, and the next day arrived.

Hunter slept in a spare room at the Major's house, the officer's wife going above and beyond in making him feel comfortable. While it felt good to actually get under clean blankets, he was up after only a few hours—and so were the Major and fifty of the townspeople.

Both men and women, they had a lot of work to do today. By the end of it, everyone involved felt they had done their best to prevent their little village from disaster.

But only time would tell if they had done enough.

The real night fell again.

Hours before the Major had assembled a second squadron of villagers—again men and women—to serve as a crude but effective early warning system.

Two were stationed on Far Beach, with binoculars on the Russian K-2 base just two miles across the fast-moving strait. They'd begun monitoring activity at the base around 10 p.m. It was shortly before midnight, though, when they heard the unmistakable rumble of jet engines warming up. Armed with a high-intensity battery lamp, they immediately began flashing a coded message up to a second team of observers stationed atop the island's jagged mountaintop.

These people were able to count the number of planes taking off from K-2. Just as Hunter had predicted, the tiff between the islands was not over. The base's four remaining Frogfoots had lifted off and were forming up for an attack on the island.

This information was sent down the other side of the mountain, this time in the form of a flashing red light. Somewhere in the murk below, a green light flashed twice on in return.

Then someone threw a switch and the curvy lines of the village's old Victorian style streetlights blinked on.

By five minutes to midnight, the quartet of Russian attack planes had made their way over from K-2 and was looping around the southern tip of the heart-shaped island.

The Frogfoots were flying slower tonight—for a disturbing reason. They weren't carrying their relatively lightweight cluster-bomb dispensers this time. Instead, each plane was lugging a pair of 500-pound iron bombs, each one capable of taking out a city block. The orders from their base commander, issued soon after his daily vodka lunch, were simple: Flatten the village and put an end to the nonsense.

With this is mind, the Frogfoots transitioned into their attack profiles, broke into two pairs and went down to 500 feet.

It was snowing as usual, but navigating by sight, the pilots of the first two attack planes spotted the familiar-looking rows of the village's amber streetlights. They immediately armed their weapons.

Going down to just 300 feet, the first two planes went in low and fast, dropping two 500-pound bombs each through the blowing snow, using the streetlights as their aiming points. There was a series of terrific explosions as all 2,000 pounds of bombs hit at once. The entire heart-shaped island shuddered from the impacts.

The second pair of attack jets came in right behind the first, perfectly mimicking their comrades' bombing run. Another ton of ordnance fell through the intense snow squall, slamming right into the remaining lines of streetlights. Once again, a string of massive explosions shook the stormy night.

Then the two attackers climbed to 2,000 feet, re-joined their colleagues, and returned to the K-2 base.

In just this one strike, the Russians had dropped more than twenty times the amount of ordnance on the village than in the last six months combined.

The message was clear: This is what happens when you mistreat Russian pilots.

Chapter Thirteen

His name was Jasper Maskelyne.

He was one of Hunter's heroes. A brilliant magician in the 1930s, Maskelyne joined the British Army when World War II broke out and was given a highly unusual assignment: using his skills as an illusionist, he was to mislead the German military wherever and whenever he could.

He took on this mission with vigor. He and his men created fake armies out of rubber tanks and trucks. They created fake radio traffic to convince the Nazis that an attack was either coming or not coming. He once blinded a formation of German bombers trying to bomb the Suez Canal by creating a mind-blowing light show with spinning mirrors and huge arc lights strung along both sides of the waterway.

But his greatest illusion was when he moved the entire Port of Alexandria one mile away from its original location, fooling German bomber pilots into dropping their weapons on the empty desert—for eight nights in a row. He did this by recreating the streetlights of the strategically important Egyptian city in the middle of a vast open field, convincing the Luftwaffe that it was their target.

Hunter nicked a little bit of Maskelyne's magic to counter a dangerous situation with a deceptively simple plan. With the help of the fifty villagers, he and the Major strung lights out on an open snow field about a half mile south of the village, recreating as best they could the pattern of street lamps in their little town.

At night, and in the blowing snow, the attacking Russian pilots couldn't tell the difference, aimed at the fake lights, and expended all their ordnance for nothing.

That's how Hunter saved the village.

But he didn't stop there.

The four Frogfoots returned to K-2, landing in pairs.

In their minds, the raid had been a success. The residents may have hidden in their bomb shelters, but their tiny village was no more. Good or bad, the pilots had fulfilled their commander's wishes.

The planes taxied to their rough parking stands and shut down their engines. A brief bit of ground crew work was done, and then everyone hurried into the drafty barracks for vodka and, hopefully, a fire in the woodstove.

The rumbling began just a minute later.

It became so loud, so quickly, the Russians thought it was an earthquake. Indeed, the old barracks was shaking—all except the floor.

They rushed to the window to see the old SAAB-21 roar over their base just twenty feet off the deck.

Its nose lit up by cannon shells and tracers, it was firing at the base's fuel tank. Five thousand gallons of aviation gas went up with a roar and a blinding ball of orange flame.

Next came the base's lone hangar. Almost an antique to begin with, it was hit by so many phosphorus-tipped tracer shells that it burst into flames almost immediately.

Behind it was the ammunition bunker. Three well-placed cannon shots went through its reinforced door and lit off all the ordnance inside. The entire island shook with the sound of another massive explosion.

The attacker did a quick loop and steered toward the four Frogfoots, conveniently lined up along the old and cracked tarmac. Another perfectly aimed five-second burst was all it took. The glowing cannon shells tore into the Russian planes, igniting them like a string of giant cherry bombs.

Another loop, and now the attacker aimed for the base's runway. For this, four 200-pound bombs dropped from its underbelly.

Once again, perfect aim, perfect timing. The attacker left four craters down the center line of the landing strip, and rendered it, just like the rest of the base, inoperable.

All this took less than thirty seconds.

But the plane took one more loop—and suddenly was heading directly for the barracks.

Everyone inside froze. The nose of the airplane lit up once more. A stream of tracer shells came right at the barracks and then . . . went over the roof.

Once again the sheer noise of the old airplane shook what was left of K-2 right down to its nuts and bolts. It screamed over the barracks and was gone.

But the message was clear. Next time, I won't miss . . .

Chapter Fourteen

The next day went by in the same dreamlike fashion that seemed to be the normal state of affairs on the heart-shaped island—but there was a new, more peaceful air to the place.

K-2 was no more. The War of The Nonsense was over, and the island returned to the small, tranquil village it yearned to be.

Just a few hours after his attack, Hunter once again took off in the SAAB-21 and was soon back over the devastated Russian outpost. He flew once over the base, low and slow, making sure those on the ground, shivering around a huge bonfire, could see him. Then he climbed to 5,000 feet and started a series of long, slow orbits above the still-smoking island letting them know he was still up there, watching them.

Two hours into this, Hunter spotted an ocean-going barge approaching K-2. The Russians began assembling near a tiny dock on the north side of the island.

They had a few crates with them, and lots of duffle bags. As he watched from above, thirty-six Russians boarded the vessel and it departed, leaving the straits and heading east, back toward Russia. Three dozen lucky men—alive only because Hunter didn't blast them to

Kingdom Come. And it was only that none of their raids had killed or maimed anyone on the heart-shaped island that he'd held his fire.

For this reason alone, his intuition was telling him that, at least in this little piece of the near-Arctic, the Russians would not return any time soon.

Once the SAAB-21 was returned to storage, Hunter and the Major drove back to the town and went directly to the tavern.

Now the place was crowded with just about the entire population of the small town. Lots of beer, lots of food, lots of interest in him, sitting with the Major at the same table as before, a small army of glasses of beer lined up before them.

Hunter ate more stew, drank more beer, and the celebration turned into a boozy haze. There were lots of women about, talking to him, buying him drinks.

But the one girl he was looking for, the stunning redhead who'd let him in the side door the night before, was nowhere in sight.

He hadn't seen her in the shelters, nor when the villagers were helping string the lights in the snow field to fool the Russians. The more beer he drank, the more he wondered if he'd just somehow made her up.

*****

Then it happened.

The celebration finally died down after many hours of revelry. The Major and his wife invited Hunter back to their house to sleep it off—and he gratefully accepted.

They helped each other out of the pub and began the short walk to the Sharp household, when suddenly Hunter stopped in mid-step and cocked his head sky-ward.

He'd gotten used to hearing the waves crashing and the sonic winds whipping through the crevices and over the mountain.

But this was a different sound.

Deep-throated. Steadily growing. Mechanical.

Getting closer . . .

The Major heard it, too.

He grabbed Hunter's arm for support.

"My God," he gasped. "Those are jet engines. They sound like Russian airplanes . . ."

Hunter knew in an instant that the Major was right. Russian airplanes were approaching the island.

But they weren't the enemy.

Just the opposite.

They went overhead not a minute later.

Two Su-34s in American markings—one loaded for bear, the other a buddy tanker.

With great surprise to himself, Hunter's heart sank to his feet.

This dream was over.

His rescuers were here.

He and the Major rushed to the hidden airbase.

The two Su-34s were in the middle of a low slow orbit over the snowy plateau. Once they saw Hunter had arrived, the flight leader dropped a canister from one of his bomb racks.

Then the two planes formed up again and disappeared to the west.

Hunter retrieved the canister and found three things inside: two IEAD modules and a plastic bottle of no-label whiskey. His favorite brand.

A note was attached to the bottle.

It read: "Same time tomorrow."

It took Hunter almost that long to do a final series of checks and last-minute adjustments to his flight systems, getting his plane ready to get back into the air.

The Major stayed with him the whole time, helping wherever he could, making coffee in the plane's tiny galley when their supply got low and adding some of the no-name whiskey when needed.

The IEAD modules dropped to Hunter fit perfectly, replacing the ones he'd transferred to the Fab 4 earlier. His engines turned over with no problem, and his instrument panel lit up and stayed that way.

He knew he had to go quickly. As the moment of his departure drew closer, he looked out the cockpit window to see that the entire population of the town had come out to the cliffside airport to see him off.

That's when it really hit him. He'd been here only a few days, but he felt like it had been years and that all these people were his friends.

And, damn, he had to go.

The two Su-34s showed up again, exactly 24 hours later.

They flew low over the island, doing double wing-wags, before going into a slow orbit above the heart-shaped island. Hunter's escort and fueling station awaited him. It was time to join them.

He did one last check of his systems and deemed himself ready to take off. He hugged the Major goodbye and helped him down the ladder out of the attack plane.

Then he strapped himself in and brought his engines up to half power.

He looked out the cockpit one last time at the crowd of villagers. Some were holding homemade American flags. Some were waving; some were even crying.

Hunter waved back to them, took a deep gulp of oxygen and tried to center his emotions. Another gulp and he went up to full power and got ready to pop the brakes.

Then he glanced back at the crowd one more time— and that's when he saw her.

Standing on the edge of the crowd was the redhead. She was wearing a winter parka, but the hood was down and she had her white baseball cap on. There was no mistaking her, curls fluttering in slow motion despite the brisk wind.

He was already in his takeoff profile; brakes popped, there was no turning back now.

He thought he saw her blow him a kiss; an instant later, his afterburners kicked in.

And then he was gone.

PART TWO

"Attack of the Bikini Pirates"

Chapter Fifteen

The battered aircraft carrier USS *USA* was 900 miles southeast of Iceland when the trio of American Su-34s came into view.

The gargantuan ex-Russian warship was still being repaired after suffering massive damage during a fierce battle on her decks not a month before. United American engineers had performed miracles in that time just keeping her afloat. Clearing the damaged flight deck alone had taken two weeks. Getting the flight elevators and ship's basic steering working again had also required thousands of man hours.

But when it came time for the Odessa Raid, the engineers took a big risk, deciding to go to sea with thousands of things, big and small, not yet fixed—including the ship's power plants. The fact that the enormous vessel was not yet able to sail under its own power didn't deter them. They simply assembled a small fleet of oceangoing tugboats to both push and pull the carrier wherever it had to go.

This was really living on the edge, and dangerously so. But the ship had an important role to play. It was the strike force's emergency recovery ship. It *had* to put to sea.

Somehow it all worked. The four other attack planes under the command of Ben Wa and JT Twomey had all been plagued with typical Russian technical problems on the way home. Luckily the tugs had been able to move the USS *USA* to a position where it could recover all of the aircraft. Otherwise they would have gone into the drink.

Two days later, the Phoenix airplane from the heart-shaped island banged in, carrying the six exhausted pilots. Since then the tugs had fiercely pushed and pulled the carrier trying to get closer to where Hunter was stranded.

It was Crunch and Elvis, Frost and Marcotte who went back for him, dropping the needed parts the day before and then escorting him to the carrier.

Now Hunter and his rescuers were circling the ship, ready to come in and land.

Hunter was asleep within ten minutes of trapping onto the carrier.

He'd barely climbed out of the plane and thanked his friends for coming back for him when he was led to a small stateroom. He collapsed onto the bunk and went into a deep slumber with no dreams that he could remember.

An entire day went by before he finally woke up. For the first few seconds, he thought he was still back inside his airplane, sitting atop the snowy cliff on the heart-shaped island.

Crunch showed up at his door a few minutes later. He had three hot meals on trays for him, plus a bottle of whiskey and a pot of coffee. Hunter inhaled the food while Crunch poured out some heavily laced coffee.

Hunter gave him the short version of what happened on the heart-shaped island after the overcrowded Fab 4 left. Then Crunch briefed him on events aboard the aircraft carrier in those same few days.

"I know you talked to Fitz," he said to Hunter. "But just to confirm, the shipyard and air base on *Sekret Ostrov* were completely incinerated. And now that you're here, it means everyone made it back in one piece. That's all good news."

But they both knew it was a lukewarm victory at best, because all indications were that Viktor had somehow escaped the attack.

And was still out there, somewhere.

But in the meantime, Crunch told him a new crisis had flared up.

"Four ships have gone missing in the mid-Atlantic over the past week," he began starkly. "One is a Free Canadian destroyer; the others are Canadian freighters. The destroyer had been escorting the freighters when they all just disappeared."

"That's a little strange," Hunter told him between bites of his second meal. "Any idea what happened to them?"

Crunch shook his head. "We've been heading south ever since you banged aboard," he replied. "The Canadians asked us for help in locating these ships. They don't have any air assets in the area and they're desperate to find their crews. After all they've done for us over the years, we couldn't say no."

Hunter was nodding profusely between bites. He wasn't even sure what he was eating.

But then he stopped in mid-chew.

"Wait—does this involve me?" he asked.

Crunch passed him his first cup of whiskey mixed with coffee.

"The Canadians asked if you could lead the aerial portion of the search," he replied. "Price of fame."

Hunter felt his heart sink. Down to every fiber of his being, all he wanted to do was get his own Su-34 in good enough shape to fly back to America. It seemed like he'd been gone for months, not just a few days. But the Free Canadians had been their loyal allies for years, so this was something he could not say no to.

It was only then that he felt the movement of the ship.

Push-pull. Push-pull . . .

Years before, he and his friends transported another aircraft carrier the same way: pushed and pulled by tugs. They'd gone through the Mediterranean and somehow reached the Suez Canal just in time for another of the almost innumerable battles against Viktor.

Push-pull . . .

Once the movement got into your head, it never left. Push-pull.

So much like life itself.

Hunter drained his cup and Crunch refilled it.

Accepting that he had one more mission to fly before he could return home, Hunter needed details.

"So where did these ships go missing exactly?" he asked Crunch.

His friend smiled. "Well, that's the best part, Hawk," he said. "Let's just say they lost their way in the general area of Bermuda."

"Please don't tell me . . ." Hunter started to say.

But Crunch was already nodding. "Do you want the coordinates?"

Hunter just shook his head. He didn't need them.

He just knew the ships had gone missing somewhere in the Bermuda Triangle.

Chapter Sixteen

When working properly, the Su-34 was a capable long-range attack plane, just as long as it didn't have to fly *that* far.

But nobody ever mistook it for a maritime search aircraft. It was simply a different kind of airplane.

Hunter knew he would need another aircraft to look for the missing Canadian ships. Something that could fly low and slow, something that was not averse to operating around water. Incredibly, an almost perfect plane for the mission was already aboard the giant aircraft carrier.

It was a Russian-built World War II-era seaplane known as the Beriev Be-4, or simply the BB-4.

It was found packed in crates deep within the carrier a few days after the United Americans took over the big flattop. The ship's engineers reassembled the aircraft as they found a seaplane was a valuable asset when they were putting the carrier through its hasty push-pull sea trials off Nantucket.

But the BB-4 was an odd bird. Just thirty feet long with a thirty-eight-foot wingspan, without its engine, the seaplane looked almost sleek from hull to tail. However, its large propeller was mounted on top of the top-mounted inverted gull wing, giving the BB-4 the impression of a hunchback.

This marriage of slick and ugly was a typical Russian design. But the little seaplane was rugged, and with extra fuel tanks it could fly more than a thousand miles. Just what it was doing aboard the aircraft carrier in the first place was still unknown.

At the beginning of Hunter's third day on the USS *USA*, he was able to crawl through the BB-4, giving it the once over. It featured a two-man cockpit, but as the co-pilot's seat could be folded back and stored away, the area around the controls was almost spacious. The topside rear gun station had been removed; however, its two 30-caliber machine guns had been mounted in the wing. The plane also had a helpful if unusual feature—a window in the flight deck floor right behind the foot pedals. This allowed the pilot to simply look down when searching for something over water.

Finally, the BB-4 was a true seaplane. Its under-fuselage was shaped like a boat, and it had stabilizing floats under each wingtip. But it had no landing gear, no wheels. To take off, the plane had to be put into the water using a small deck crane mounted on the open fantail of the carrier.

Hunter was ready to go by 0900 hours.

They had rendezvoused with another Canadian warship just off the northern coast of Bermuda and shared maps of the area.

Actually, a collection of five main islands and dozens of smaller ones, Bermuda had yet to recover from World War III. At one time a tropical paradise and tourist destination, Bermuda was now a home to outlaws, smugglers, pirates, and, some claimed, other-worldly activity. There had been no semblance of government or law and order there in years.

The three missing freighters had been sailing north in a small convoy when they suddenly disappeared off St. George's Island, one of the largest in the Bermuda chain. The Free Canadian destroyer escorting them vanished, too.

The last person to see the convoy was a self-described sea witch who lived on a smaller island just off St. George. She claimed the four ships disappeared into a strange fog about ten miles east of her location. The Free Canadian military made contact with her, debriefed her, and passed the info on to the United Americans.

At the end of her testimony, though, she'd added this chilling addendum: "Most of Bermuda is haunted, and things disappear here all the time."

The plan was simple.

Now that the aircraft carrier had arrived, it would launch the four Ka-25 double-rotor naval helicopters it had on board to search the waters surrounding Bermuda.

Two Su-34s would launch and do some high-altitude photo recon to see if their cameras picked up anything unusual. The on-site Canadian warship would circumnavigate the islands, looking for clues closer in to shore.

That left searching the inner part of the island chain to Hunter.

The BB-4 was the ideal plane for this. Bermuda was overflowing with bays, harbors, channels, straits—and islands. More than 150 of them.

Hunter could fly low over these places, executing his own one-man search plan, checking each and every island—and hoping to do it all in one day.

But as always in things like this, there was a complicating factor.

A large weather system was stirring in the lower Caribbean. It was expected to build into a monstrous hurricane and move up the East Coast within the next 24 hours.

So, the clock was ticking.

Crunch helped Hunter get strapped inside the little seaplane. Hunter had his trusty M-16 and his .357 Magnum and plenty of ammunition with him. He couldn't imagine a scenario in which he would have to use the hardware. But that's exactly why he'd brought it.

"What's your feeling on this?" Crunch asked him as he prepared to have the tiny seaplane lowered over the side.

Hunter could only shrug. "Those ships are out there somewhere," he said. "Things don't just disappear."

Crunch lit his cigar and replied: "You did."

Five minutes later, the crew lowered the BB-4 into the sea.

Hunter started the massive top-wing engine and it replied with a cough of black smoke. It took a minute for the old prop-job to finally run true, but eventually it settled down to a loud purr.

As Hunter started to taxi away from the carrier and into the warm waters of nearby Achilles Bay, Crunch made his way up to the flat top's bridge.

The Russians built the former *Isakov* to be highly automated, but most of this equipment had been destroyed in the recent battle. The United American engineers had resurrected all the crucial controls, but many of them were now manual and held together with duct tape. The tugboats really steered the ship.

Push-pull. That's how it goes.

Crunch grabbed a coffee and watched Hunter take off. The little seaplane roared along the coral blue waves before getting airborne and going into a picture-perfect ascent. Rising steadily, it began a wide, slow orbit around the carrier.

That's when Hunter made a routine radio call to the bridge, reporting that all was well and that he was beginning his search.

Then he flew into the light overcast to the east . . . and disappeared.

Chapter Seventeen

Hunter had made that one routine call to the bridge, and that was it. The carrier's comm shack had tried to reach him hundreds of times since, putting out a message every 10 minutes, hoping they'd get some kind of reply.

But it never happened.

The search for the missing ships was immediately expanded to look for the Wingman. All of the carrier's planes and choppers were mustered. They flew vast ocean grid patterns in round-the-clock shifts. All kinds of night vision and infrared scopes were employed. Even the push-pull tugboats were deployed, detaching from their tow ropes and dispersing in all directions to search the surface of the sea.

But nothing was found.

No wreckage, no oil slick. Nothing.

Hunter had simply vanished.

Strangely, several people had spotted him after that last radio call.

About twenty minutes after he took off, one of the carrier's Kasov helicopters saw Hunter's odd little seaplane flying low over Lighthouse Hill on St George's Island.

Knowing that the carrier had lost contact with him, the copter pilots tried calling Hunter directly. He never responded, but he did wag his wings when he and the copter briefly crossed paths around 3,000 feet before Hunter banked into a nearby cloud.

About an hour later, one of the Su-34s, taking pictures fifty miles off the west coast of Bermuda's Main Island, picked up Hunter's flying boat on the edge of one of its video feeds. It appeared for only a few moments, but it was definitely the weird little Russian seaplane, flying almost at wave-top level at high speed.

Like the copter's airmen before them, the Su-34 pilots tried contacting Hunter on the radio.

But they never got a reply.

Consequently, the large weather system had started to race up the East Coast, building into a hurricane. The carrier, already being kept together by glue and prayers, had sprung so many leaks and suffered so many major electronic system failures that it had to get into port before it was caught in the storm.

So with heavy hearts, the carrier and its tugboat escorts eventually turned west and headed for Port Norfolk in what used to be Virginia.

A few hours after they safely reached the harbor, and as the hurricane roared up the coastline, the word went out to the civilized parts of America that Hawk Hunter, the Wingman, after literally coming back from the dead not a year before, was missing again.

Chapter Eighteen

There was a knock, the door opened, and the two blonde and barefoot bikini-clad girls walked into the huge bedroom.

One was carrying a tray of fruit and Johnny Bread, the other a pot of tea.

Hawk Hunter rolled over in the massive waterbed and wiped the sleep from his eyes.

"Breakfast is served, I guess," he muttered.

The girls put the tray and tea in front of him and then pulled back the curtains to let the early-morning sunshine in. The huge storm had blown through during the night; lots of rain, lots of wind, but moving quickly off to the north. He'd slept through most of it.

One girl freshened-up the water in the Jacuzzi. The other checked to make sure the bar was well-stocked.

"Eat, bath, then a drink?" one of the beauties asked him.

Hunter sat up, bunching the satin sheets above his midsection.

"Sounds great," he replied.

The second blonde ran her fingers through his long-ish hair.

"And I can trim that up for you if you want," she cooed.

But he could barely speak at this point.

"Sure, maybe this afternoon," he finally spit out.

Both girls smiled, and like models leaving a runway, exited the room.

Hunter let out a whistle of relief and collapsed back onto his pillows.

"How long before I get tired of this?" he wondered.

There had never been a time in his life when he'd wanted to write a book about his adventures. He'd always been too busy actually living them to stop everything and start scribbling it all down.

But this time was different. This time he'd had the urge to start taking notes because anything that started out this strangely usually just got even stranger. He wanted to make sure he remembered it all.

As for a title, he already had one: "Attack of the Bikini Pirates." It would be impossible to call it anything else.

But where would he begin?

Should he start with him finding the missing ships? Or the strange little paradise he now found himself in? Or how the winds had so suddenly turned demonic, blowing his little seaplane so far off course even he didn't know where he was?

Or how all that happened in the span of just a few minutes?

And who would believe it?

It was that crazy wind from nowhere that he really couldn't understand.

He'd left the USS *USA* with no problems. Everything was normal with his flight, except that his radio kept crapping out. He'd sent a dozen messages back to the carrier. None was answered. Nor had any of their radio calls reached him.

But the storm was coming, and time was of the essence. So he had continued his search, not wanting to turn around, go back to the carrier, land on the water, have them pick him up with the crane, put him back inside the ship, fix the radio, then return him to the water and start all over again.

If he found the missing ships, he knew he'd have had no problem returning to the carrier and informing the crew that the mystery had been solved.

Or so he'd thought.

Other than all that, the first few hours of his search had been uneventful. He flew over dozens of small

Bermudan islands, looking for any sign of the missing ships but finding none.

He'd spotted some of the other search craft in that time and signaled them when he could. In between, he'd kept a close eye on the changing weather conditions to the south. Several scattered thunderheads appeared first, but within just a couple of hours their clouds had spread across the entire southern horizon. Once they'd started to coalesce and formed into a spiral pattern, he didn't need a weatherman to tell him which way the wind was blowing.

The storm had grown into a monster and was heading right for him.

His fuel was down to just an hour when he found himself flying along the east coast of Horseshoe Bay, Bermuda. It was almost time to head back to the carrier when a gust of wind began pushing him northeast, into an enormous fog bank, something the outer Bermudian islands were famous for.

He fought the wind for almost five minutes, trying to steer the little flying boat back onto his search pattern, but it proved a losing battle. The gale was stronger than anything he'd ever experienced. Because of his fuel situation, he was forced to let it take him, hoping he could get back on course after the gusts died down.

When the mysterious wind finally let him go, though, he was at least a hundred miles from where he wanted to be, flying at about 2,000 feet in extremely foggy conditions, with no land he could see anywhere.

Now the fog became the biggest problem. It was so thick he couldn't get a fix on any horizon. And the old plane's compass wouldn't stop moving, even for a moment. At times he didn't know if he was flying straight ahead—or straight down.

Maybe *this* is what happens in the Bermuda Triangle, he'd thought. You're lost in the fog forever. He couldn't help it. The atmospherics were that screwy.

He went on to burn through even more fuel just flying around, trying to get his bearings. This was not like him. Whenever he was airborne, he *always* knew where he was.

But not this time.

He had to gradually lose altitude and hope the mist thinned out before he went in with a splash. He started flying in a wide circle and, bit by bit, began to descend, looking through the window below his feet. All this took even more time and fuel—but he finally spotted wave tops and leveled off at fifty feet.

At last he could see the horizon, though it was cloud-covered in all directions. He needed to go west to return to the carrier. He consulted the jittery compass and turned toward what he thought was the right direction, but everything inside him started telling him he was actually heading east. When he did a long 180-degree loop, his instincts began screaming again, insisting he was heading north. He went on like this for another ten minutes, turning every which way, hoping he'd find something his brain could be comfortable with.

But that never happened, either. When the old BB-4's compass started spinning 360s, he knew he was in serious trouble.

He found the missing ships a moment later.

Chapter Nineteen

Hunter poured himself more tea and ate another piece of Johnny Bread.

The sun was pouring into the bedroom now, heating up the silk sheets, making everything feel even more tropical.

He looked down at his arms. Both were scratched from the wrists to the shoulders, as was his chest. He'd been flying most of his life and had been in his fair share of air crashes, but nothing like the one he was in shortly after finding the missing ships.

He'd found himself down to just twenty feet and was still whacking the side of the cockpit compass when he flew right over them. Three freighters and a Free Canadian destroyer painted in dark gray sea camo—all of them anchored in a small bay, just barely visible in the fog.

He saw them for only an instant through his floor window. An instant after that, he plowed into a grove of palm trees, shearing off their tops with the plane's hulled bottom. The resulting debris flew up and over the canopy and right into his engine.

The propeller fouled immediately and started to kick. And even though he tried mightily, he couldn't keep the plane from going into a dive.

Luckily, though, the grove ended at the edge of a large lagoon. Unluckily, there was a heavily armed gunboat anchored right in the middle of it.

He hit the water at about ninety knots, nose pointed right at the gunboat. With impact imminent, he yanked back on the controls, buried the throttle, and hoped for the best.

The engine coughed loudly, but the plane lifted off the water's surface—briefly. He clipped the gunboat's mast and cut off all its antennas along with some kind of weapon that had been mounted on the top deck.

Then the plane hit the water again, very hard this time. The prop finally succumbed to the strain and the palm branches, backfiring twice and then fluttering dead. He bounced once, very high, slammed back down, bounced again, and then came down for good, only to skid along the shallow water, careen off a wooden dock, and catapult onto the foggy beach itself.

When he finally came to rest, the plane's nose was stuck in the side of a tall sand dune, twenty feet in from the lagoon and not more than 200 feet from the wounded gunboat.

Taking his weapons with him, he scrambled out of the mangled cockpit, scratching his arms and chest in the process. He could hear angry voices coming from the boat, but there was so much fog around, he was able to plunge into the jungle and leave the area quickly.

It was only then that he realized the daylight was fading. Here for at least one night, he knew he had to find his way back to the missing ships, just to make sure they were real.

This meant taking the long way around the lagoon and finding the palm tree grove he'd given the trim to. He knew it would be a long, sweaty trudge.

He suffered even more scratches fighting the thick jungle. By the end of it, his arms and chest looked like he'd lost a fight to a cat.

After moving through the misty forest for about a half hour, he came upon a clearing ringed by an old chain link fence.

On the other side was a farm of huge tuba-shaped ground vents pumping out vast quantities of . . . fog. There were at least a hundred of these weird retractable vents, and he could clearly hear the hum of their attendant machinery running underground.

None of this made sense until he found a rusted sign that read, "Foggy Bum Cay Atmospheric Research

Center, U.S. Navy." He knew it was a bullshit name. This was an old black-ops site, built with 1960s technology. At some point the Navy must have needed the island to become invisible and started manufacturing continuous clouds of fog to hide it, in a part of the ocean that featured frequent fog banks.

Very James Bond.

Now someone had resurrected the site and was again taking advantage of its ground cloud-making capabilities.

But who?

And why did they snatch the four ships?

He plunged back into the jungle and began moving again.

When he finally reached the other side of the lagoon, he found the small bay where the four missing ships were anchored. It took him a few moments to pick them out in the mist. The fog was very thick here, plus it was getting dark, giving everything an eerie feel. And the monster storm was still coming.

He moved along the tree line, getting as close to the ships as he could. But suddenly he heard footsteps behind him. Lots of them. When he froze, the noise stopped.

That's when he looked down at his feet and saw a pair of huge eyes, like those belonging to a giant insect, staring up at him from a deep hole.

He remembered two things happening next. The sound of footsteps crashing through the jungle started up again and became more intense. And something reached out, grabbed his foot, and pulled him into the pit.

The hole was about eight feet deep—he had both his M-16 and .357 out before he hit the bottom. It was dark inside, but not so dark that he couldn't see a gun muzzle pointing right back at him.

Then someone whispered: "Forces Spéciales Canadiennes Libre."

He immediately lowered his weapons.

Free Canadian Special Forces. . .

Thank God, he thought. A friend.

The man indicated they should be quiet. Seconds later a multitude of footsteps went right over their heads. They belonged to at least a couple of dozen people, none of whom was trying to be stealthy. They sounded more like a mob. When it was quiet again, he and his rescuer began speaking in whispers.

"Major Hawk Hunter, United American Naval Air Force," he said, shaking hands with his host.

A small light came on and Hunter could see they were in a deep, but otherwise typical, SAS-style observation dugout complete with a camo roof. This was a place where special forces soldiers could lie in wait for days, even weeks, watching something, all while being invisible.

His host was wearing sea camos and an oversized SF helmet complete with night vision goggles and EAEs, enhanced audio emulators, bug-like "super ears." They could pick up conversations more than two miles away.

But the man couldn't stop staring at him.

He knew why. He'd been recognized.

"I'm just as surprised as you are," he told the man.

The man shook his hand again. "Captain Colin Orr," he said. "123rd Special Battalion Free Canada."

"And our friends who just walked overhead?"

Orr smiled. "Are you ready for this? An all-female army of pirates."

He was *not* ready to hear that. "Are you joking?"

"*L'armee Bikini,*" Orr said shaking his head. "The Bikini Army."

The dugout had an electronic periscope sticking out of the top. Heavily camouflaged, it gave the place 360-degree visuals.

Orr told him to look through the eyepiece. He did and saw at least two dozen women walking away from the hidden dugout and toward the captured ships. All of them were carrying automatic weapons, and all of them were indeed wearing bikinis.

"So we've died and gone to heaven?" he said, eyes still on the eyepiece.

"It's all this fog," Orr replied. "I've been listening in on these girls for almost a week with the EAEs. There's about 200 of them on the island, and they all say the same thing: There's so much moisture in the air, the humidity is unbearable. So they dress in brief swimsuits."

Eyes never leaving the scope, he asked: "Can you tell me how you got here?"

Orr indicated that they should sit down.

"I hope you like long stories," he said.

Chapter Twenty

Orr was the security officer for the lost Canadian warship, the FCS *Shag Harbor.*

Just by fate, he'd been on transfer duty from the Canadian Special Forces when the destroyer started its fateful voyage.

It had been escorting the three freighters because they were filled with second-market combat weapons bought by the Canadian military in the wild postwar black markets of Havana. Due to the sensitivity of the mission, the Free Canadian Special Forces thought it best that Orr go along.

But just as they were passing Bermuda, the ships sailed into the enormous fog bank, scattering the small convoy. In this thick mist, first one, then all three freighters were boarded by pirates. The invaders took advantage of the confusion among the crews caused by the fact that their ships were being assaulted by skimpily clad but heavily armed women. They quickly disarmed the shocked crewmen and ripped out all their radios.

By the time the *Shag Harbor* found the three ships in the fog, the pirates were threatening to kill the crews if the destroyer took any offensive action or sent out any calls for help.

"In other words," Orr told him, "the queen took the king. Game. Set. Match."

He explained that the four ships were led to the island, never once getting out of the thick vapor. It was only after they'd entered the small bay that the *Shag's* sailors even realized their captors were all women. A band of female pirates. And they all tended to wear . . . brief swimsuits.

"I couldn't make this stuff up if I tried," Orr told him.

The pirates had been operating in this area for the past year, using or selling what they captured, quietly ransoming crews back to whomever they belonged, all while hiding underneath a continuous layer of artificial fog of their own making. While most of the planet was at war, the bikini pirates had become the unlikely scourge of the north Caribbean, luring ships between here and the Bahamas into their fog banks and then robbing them.

"As soon as we saw what was going on, the captain told me to jump ship, establish a position on shore, and try to get a message out," Orr went on. "So I swam ashore. The ladies had our ships anchor here. They destroyed all of the *Shag's* communication equipment. Then everyone was blindfolded and taken off. I saw it all—and heard it all—hiding in here."

"And getting a message out?" he asked him.

"Zero luck so far," Orr said, holding up a small satellite phone. "They might have some kind of jammer working nearby. Or there's a big-ass antenna out there somewhere. Something is screwing with the ethers."

It took a few moments for all this to sink in. He was the Wingman and he'd lived a very unusual life already—but this was right up there. His second strange island in as many weeks; an army of bikini pirates? And he'd thought finding a bunch of British people off Scandinavia was weird.

"But things have changed in the few days we've been here," Orr went on. "Despite everything, these ladies seemed to be a happy bunch. But something happened about forty-eight hours ago. Suddenly they started combat training, building fortifications along the beaches near their main base, lookouts posted to the highest trees."

"That's never a good sign," he said. "What are they expecting?"

Orr just shrugged. "Something from the east . . . something not so fun. My guess is the top pirates are keeping it a secret from the rest of the ladies, but that's all I know, right now, anyway."

He returned to the periscope and watched the company of bikini-clad warriors board the captured ships and perform a cursory search. He knew they were most likely looking for him.

Despite their skimpy style of dress, they looked all business, their AK-47s and bandoliers proving the point.

"Who runs all this?" he asked Orr, eyes still glued to the scope.

The Canadian soldier laughed at that. "I was saving the best for last," he said. "Ever hear the name 'Robotov?' "

He looked back at Orr in mild shock. Everyone knew that name.

"*Viktor* Robotov?" he asked. "He's behind this?"

But Orr shook his head.

"Not Viktor," he replied. "His daughter, Viktoria. She's the queen bee around here."

Chapter Twenty-One

He and Orr cooked up the scheme that had landed him here—in the huge water bed, between silk sheets, eating breakfast and due for a drink and a hot tub soon.

It all started when he gave himself up.

He'd climbed out of the hidden hole, walked toward the captured ships, crash helmet on, hands held high.

L'armee Bikini spotted him immediately, disarmed him and took him into custody.

Night fell as he was being transported to the pirates' main base, which was on the eastern edge of the large lagoon. It was an elaborate mess of a place. Lit by blazing tiki torches, it looked to be half fort and half beach club. But it was teeming with armed women and big weapons were installed everywhere.

The harbor fronting it was filled with attack boats, mostly fifty-ton Toralla Tormentors, all of them brimming with deck guns, anti-ship missiles, and torpedoes. There were a dozen in all, and these were what the pirates used to raid shipping throughout the upper Caribbean.

Orr had been right on the money. All of the pirates' boats were at anchor; their crews working at a feverish pitch despite the evening murk and fog, building fortifications around the harbor and their base.

The vibe of impending battle was everywhere.

He was brought to the pirates' headquarters, the center of which was a large main hall that had once been a beachfront restaurant.

The hall itself was something out of a comic book. There was a bizarrely regal, post-apocalyptic look to it. A throne was set on a six foot, red-carpeted riser; many female pirates were sprawled on its steps. Others served as guards. Still more women in skimpy outfits were lounging around the hall's perimeter; others were off whispering in the dark corners. It was a pirates' version of a royal court—and intrigue was in the air.

One of his captors announced the details of his surrender, and then he was led into the hall. His captors never tied his hands or restrained him in any way. They didn't feel the need, he guessed—and they were right.

He wasn't planning on escaping.

They brought him to the foot of the throne, a guard on each side.

Only then did he get a good look at the queen sitting on the lavishly gaudy throne.

Oh no . . .

He'd actually gasped, something he didn't do too often.

So much had gone down since the raid on Viktor's secret island that he couldn't really remember what order it had happened in. Just that all of it had been very weird.

But nothing like this . . .

Because Viktoria, his archenemy's daughter, was crazy gorgeous.

Raven-hair, porcelain skin, giant azure eyes, ruby red lips. She was dressed in a short leather tunic and high black boots, knives stuck in her belt. She was even wearing a tri-corner hat with a feather sticking out of the brim. Everything but the parrot.

With a practiced noble air, she'd looked down at him and studied him for a moment.

But then she gasped, too.

She knew who he was.

"My God, you're alive?" she exclaimed.

"So far," he replied.

A buzz went around the court, word passing that the legendary Wingman was suddenly in their midst. But it was the reaction of their queen that really got tongues wagging. It was very uncharacteristic. Viktoria was rarely startled or surprised.

The pirate queen regained her composure, adjusting the feather in her cap.

"Why would Hawk Hunter surrender—to anyone?"

"We can speak here," he replied. "Or in private."

Another titter went around the room. What was he suggesting?

"Anything you want to say, you can say in front of my friends," Viktoria told him, trying not to smile.

"OK—I ask you to free the crews of the ships you snatched," he'd told her simply.

Laughter echoed around the big hall.

"And what could I possibly get in return?" Viktoria asked him.

He pointed to himself and said: "Let them go and I will remain as your prisoner."

She stood up and smiled mischievously.

"And that benefits me how?" she asked.

"You might get more of a ransom for me," he replied.

She walked down the steps toward him. The closer she got to him, the more striking she became. Reaching the floor, she stood close to him. He tried to stay calm, but it was not an easy thing to do.

"Well, Major Hunter," she said, so near he could smell a mix of rum and perfume. "What if this is not a ransom situation here?"

And that was the curveball. He couldn't take his eyes off her, and he couldn't think of anything to say.

She had him.

"Take this prisoner to the special holding cell," she called over her shoulder, never taking her eyes off him. "I'll deal with him later."

Chapter Twenty-Two

Hunter finished his breakfast, took his tub, and got dressed.

Another knock came to his door. This time a woman in a tight blue combat uniform came in. She was wearing a ski mask; it covered all but her eyes. Odd attire for the humid island and a long way, fashion-wise, from her bikini-clad associates.

She virtually ignored Hunter, instead scanning the bedroom making sure all was secure. Once convinced of this, she stepped aside—and Viktoria walked in.

Gone was the R-rated pirate costume. Now she was wearing a long satin morning gown, very luxurious, very see-through.

Hunter felt a jolt of excitement go through him. He couldn't help it. She was the progeny of history's worst criminal. Yet she was absolutely mesmerizing.

She nodded to her masked security officer. The woman hesitated for a moment, but somewhat reluctantly left them alone.

Viktoria glided over to the window seat and sat down. Hunter joined her. Outside, some of her pirates were picking up debris from the passing storm while others continued working on the beachfront base's fortifications, moving like ghosts in the fog.

Sitting so close to him, and wearing those clothes, Viktoria looked a lot younger and, again, not at all like the daughter of a notorious war criminal. But she also looked very worried.

"What has surprised you the most since you've been here?" she asked him in a slight Russian accent. "The fog?"

He almost smiled. "I think it's that you KO'd my proposal so quickly."

She looked out at the misty sea.

"But I was being honest with you," she said. "We didn't take those freighters for ransom. We took them because we needed the weapons they were carrying. And we took the destroyer because we need a warship."

"Trouble in paradise?"

She nodded gravely. "In a few days, a large, well-equipped enemy is going to come over that horizon," she said, pointing to the east. "And we're going to have a very hard time stopping them for more than a minute or so."

Curveball number two.

"What do they want here?"

She gave a slight shrug. "Our business. Our little pirating operation."

Hunter looked out on the beachfront base again. In the scheme of things Viktoria's little pirating operation was just that: little. Meanwhile, the world was awash in large military groups, state-sponsored armies and mercenary gangs. There were numerous wars going on around the globe. What was happening here was minuscule by comparison.

"But why are they picking on you?" he asked. "There's got to be bigger fish out there."

She smiled sadly. "Would you believe it's a family thing?"

He nodded. "I've met other members of your family, so . . ."

She laughed—and touched his knee.

"Well, you haven't met this one," she said.

Hunter had to think a moment. He'd tangled with Viktor many times. And just recently two of his sons.

Who was left?

"Your . . . mother?" he finally asked.

Viktoria smiled again, but this time more darkly.

"Good guess," she said, nervously playing with her hair. "And believe me, she's the *really* crazy one in our family."

"Is it OK if I'm skeptical?"

Another sad laugh, her hand still resting on his knee. Her familiarity was disarming.

"It's in our DNA," she said, as if not for the first time. "That's really my only excuse. Growing up I was well aware of the meaning of *neblagopoluchnoy*. 'Dysfunctional' to you. Russians have been using that term since before the United States was even born."

She looked up at him. "But I also believe in good fortune. Either that or it was divine intervention that brought you here. Sometimes it's hard to tell the difference."

He thought a moment, suddenly realizing there might be a bigger problem in the making here.

"But if your mother takes over this place, then she'll probably take over all of Bermuda," he said. "If that happens, she could use it as a launching pad for attacks on America."

"I'm sure that's part of her long-range plan," Viktoria replied.

Hunter felt a deep anger building inside him. Good fortune or divine intervention? It really didn't matter. Whatever was going on here, he now had to do something to stop it.

"Is your father involved in this?" he asked. The man he and his friends just flew halfway around the world to kill—and missed.

"He doesn't have to be," she said. "My mother has her own army, her own weapons, probably her own nukes."

Nukes. That was a dirty word he never wanted to hear. Another shudder went through him, and it was nowhere as pleasant as the last. A nuke base off the East Coast was not something America needed ever—and especially not now.

"What's her total force look like?"

Viktoria's lips contorted a bit, screwing up in slight confusion.

"That's hard to explain," she confessed. "We think she has a fleet of huge airplanes, but they don't really fly. They're more like ocean liners."

She used her finger to draw an outline on the window. Indeed, it looked like an enormous airplane riding atop the water.

"And their engines are up here," she said, drawing eight engines attached to a relatively small secondary wing sticking out of the fuselage just behind the cockpit.

That's when Hunter felt a third chill go through him.

The biggest one yet.

Ekranoplans.

These were thoroughly Russian weapons, and Viktoria had described them perfectly. An Ekranoplan looked like a huge airliner; its wingspan alone was wider than a football field. But in reality it was a ship, one that could fly very fast just a few feet above the surface of the water. Its secret was using the thrust from its huge engines to bounce off the water just below it, creating a cushion effect similar to the principle of hovercrafts, but on a grander, jet-powered scale.

And they were giants—almost 300 tons each. But they could travel at nearly 400 knots and carry hundreds of troops and many large weapons atop the outer fuselage, including terrifying P-280 anti-ship missiles that worked just as effectively against land targets.

These beasts were originally tested in the Caspian Sea, so they were known to militaries around the world as Caspian Sea Monsters.

"How do you know all this?" he asked her.

A tear slowly made its way down her cheek. "About two months ago, I started getting shortwave radio messages from my mother," she said. "She told me exactly what she was planning to do, and she knew I was too weak to stop her. I didn't pay too much attention to her because she gets into the bottle every so often."

She brushed her cheek and sniffed.

"But then a week ago, one of our gunboats had an engine blow out coming back from a raid," she continued. "It drifted for hours before it was fixed. But just before they got underway again, the crew spotted something on the eastern horizon. It looked like a floating harbor, but it was mammoth-sized. More like a floating city. It had two support ships alongside plus at least a half-dozen giant 'flying boats.' "

"To the untrained eye, that's exactly what an Ekranoplan looks like," he said. "Where did they see it?"

"About fifty miles due east of here," Viktoria replied. "But that's the extent of our intelligence—and it's a week old."

She further explained that, after the taunts from her mother, spotting the floating dock prompted her to turn her pirate army into a defensive force.

"That's when we began preparing the fortifications," she explained, "while raiding ships we hoped had weapons and ammunition aboard."

She looked out the window to the fog-covered beach nearby.

"My people are fighters," she said softly. "And they know their stuff. And we've been training around the clock since we first learned this was a serious threat. But we can never defeat an attacking force like that."

She looked him in eye. "So that's the deal I have to make," she said. "You help me against my mother—and then I'll let everyone go. You included."

"And if I don't agree?"

She got up to go.

"Surely someone like you has read this book before," she said, briefly stroking his cheek with her fingers. "If you don't help me, I'll have to kill you all."

Timing really was everything, because not a half minute after Viktoria left, Hunter heard a faint beeping coming from his crash helmet.

He retrieved the bone dome and reached deep inside its thick foam padding. Within was a three-inch-long, half-inch-thick, flexible walkie-talkie. He pushed a small red button on the top and the beeping stopped. He opened the communication link.

Captain Orr was on the other end.

"She's not eaten you, I take it?" he asked.

"Maybe she's not hungry yet," Hunter replied.

Orr had been working his super-ears since Hunter gave himself up; the mini-me walkie-talkie was one of its remote devices. The Canadian was hiding in the jungle a quarter mile to the south. It took many hours and some fine tuning, but from this vantage point, he was finally able to isolate Viktoria's voice, one among dozens. He'd heard the entire exchange between Hunter and the pirate queen just minutes ago, as well as conversations before and even now afterward.

"Want the short version?" he asked Hunter.

"Yes—please . . ."

"She's scared, Hawk," Orr told him. "They're all scared. If anything, she soft-pedaled the situation to you. Her mother has been radioing her four, five times a day for weeks. Taunting her. Nagging her. Just tearing her down—all in perfect English, by the way. Some of it was particularly nasty."

"How so?" Hunter asked.

"As in Mom doesn't want to waste a nuke blowing up her daughter's sad little pirate base. And Mommy vows to kill all her 'girlfriends' and then send Vikki to a prison in Siberia—forever."

"Looks like our friend has both daddy *and* mommy issues," Hunter said.

"And she knows when the invaders appear, it's going to be a short fight," Orr added.

"Did she say that before or after talking to me?" Hunter asked him.

"Before *and* after," Orr replied. "In fact, she just said it to her security girlfriend."

Hunter sat on the edge of the huge waterbed, causing it to slosh around. "That's not encouraging," he said.

"And if she's serious about her mother having a half-dozen Ekranoplans, well . . . one of them carries enough firepower to take out this foggy little dot in about two minutes," Orr said. "I can't imagine what six could do. Their biggest problem might be finding their way around in all this soup. And our little destroyer isn't going to stop them for more than a few seconds."

Hunter rubbed his eyes. At that point, he felt like climbing back in bed.

"Well, you know her counteroffer," he said to Orr. "She'll let us go if we help her. Did you hear anything that indicates it might be a fix?"

"My training says she seems sincere in private conversation," Orr replied. "Plus, I think she thinks it's a lost cause, no matter what."

"Then it's not a difficult choice," Hunter said. "We've got to go along with her, at least for now."

"Agreed," Orr said. "Especially because we're all stuck here, and that means their fight is our fight."

"Will your guys on the ship buy in?"

"When I tell them the circumstances—and that you are here—they'll all go along with us. The freighter crews will do what they can, too, I'm sure. But still, our ship is only a destroyer. Two seven-inch guns and a few torpedoes. If they see us coming, one of those Ekranoplans could put an end to it pretty quick."

Hunter knew the Canadian wasn't kidding. This wasn't David versus Goliath. It was David versus Godzilla.

"Then we've got to make sure of at least one thing," he said wearily. "That they don't see us coming . . ."

*****

Hunter climbed into his battle gear and put the radio back into his helmet.

Then he knocked twice on the door. A female guard opened it for him.

"I think Viktoria will want to talk to me," he told her.

Five minutes later, he was back in the great hall, but the place had emptied out. Only Viktoria's security officer and the pirate queen herself remained. They were both sitting on the top step of throne's riser, dejectedly sharing a bottle of wine. The security officer pulled down her mask as soon as he was led in.

Viktoria was surprised to see him—he could tell. She stood up and immediately came down the stairs to meet him, her silk gown flowing behind her.

"You've wasted no time in making your decision," she said. "I hope you made . . ."

But he held up his hand and gently interrupted her. "Because we don't have any time to waste," he said. "I'll help you, but on two conditions."

Her face brightened for a moment. "And they are?"

"The Canadians will stay here and fight with us," he replied. "And you can keep the freighters' cargo, but you'll have to give them back their ships when it's over."

145

He heard the breath catch in her throat.

"And?"

"And," Hunter told her, "we'll need a couple of bags of coins, preferably gold ones."

Now she did laugh. "What makes you think we have bags of gold coins?"

He just shrugged. "You're pirates, aren't you?"

Chapter Twenty-Three

Night fell on Foggy Bum Cay.

With an extra layer of the manufactured fog aiding them, the destroyer *Shag Harbor* pulled out of the hidden anchorage and steered east.

The Free Canadian crew was back on board, 123 men released per Hunter's agreement. Orr was among them, as was the captain, Fred "Gerry" Cheevers, who was a friend of Hunter's good friend Rene Frost of the Free Canadian Air Force.

Hanging off a crane on the destroyer's stern was Hunter's hastily repaired BB-4 seaplane. The strange little aircraft was extensively beaten up and the engine still had a mouthful of sliced palm fronds. But it still worked and its gas tanks were again full. Bringing it along was essential to what they hoped to do.

Viktoria had tried but failed to locate where her mother's daily taunts were broadcasting from. As the messages were transmitted over shortwave, they could be coming from just about anywhere. But they were also blocked from receiving replies thanks to some kind of jamming device. So Viktoria's mother's rants were one-way streams, making them even more infuriating.

The only real piece of intelligence they had was the approximate location of the enormous floating harbor a week ago; that was the very thin thread they were out here chasing tonight. If they were going to be successful, the Canadian warship would have to find the sea-going marina—and quickly.

That's where the battered BB-4 came in. Once the destroyer cleared the massive bank of artificial fog about fifteen miles out from the island, it came to a brief stop, just long enough for the crew to use its crane to lower Hunter and the seaplane over the side.

He took off at exactly midnight, an extra wet and rough ascent as the sea was getting choppy. The night was clear though. No moon and billions of stars. Perfect for his night vision goggles.

Once airborne, Hunter gave the destroyer a wag of the wings and the small warship began moving again.

Meanwhile, Hunter turned east and started searching for something that was just one step away from being a phantom.

It was times like this that Hunter was forced to rely on his instincts again—and his substantial, if curious, ESP capability.

To him, everything came from feel. If a compass told him he was heading north but the feeling inside told him it was south, he would turn around—and go with his heart. It wasn't rocket science to him; it was just the way it was.

He'd become one with every airplane he'd ever climbed into. His ride for many years was an F-16XL Cranked Arrow fighter, until he wrecked it landing on the fouled flight deck of the then-*Isakov* at the height of the battle for her. Nothing would equal the bond he'd had with that aircraft. True, he'd flirted with the Su-34, though now he knew she was a temperamental mistress. But everything else he'd flown over these years always had some kind of feel to it—even this stubby little flying boat.

Under these conditions, and whenever he was in flight, his mind was like an early warning system. He knew if there were any airplanes in his vicinity and their locations, all without looking at his radar screen. What's more, the vibes almost always led him toward his objective. He was counting on the same kind of magic tonight.

Once he was at 2,000 feet with the cumulus bank of fake fog far behind him, he gripped the BB-4's controls just a bit tighter and closed his eyes. As always, his mind went to another place. But this time, it traveled back to the heart-shaped island and the Major and the bar patrons and the volunteers who'd helped him put an end to the mindless Russian harassment.

It seemed like it had all happened years ago, when actually it had been less than a week. Too cold there, too muggy here, he thought. Maybe he'd get it right someday. But then he realized he simply missed the chilly place and its warm engaging people. Nothing cosmic about that.

He flew along like this for quite a while; he could never be exactly sure of the time. But suddenly his head was filled with a green glow, even though his eyes were still shut. He opened them slowly and found the emerald flare of night vision almost blinding him. His see-in-the-dark goggles were picking up a huge heat source straight ahead.

He adjusted his focus and saw, ten miles off his airplane's nose, a huge floating harbor anchored along with two attendant support ships with a half-dozen Ekranoplans tied up to it. But it was like something from a dream. It was enormous, and as Viktoria said, looked more like a floating city.

But at least he'd found it.

He let out a long whistle of relief.

The *feeling* had worked again.

Five minutes later, he was flirting with 20,000 feet, the absolute ceiling for the tiny seaplane.

He wasn't too hot anymore. With no pressurization and his canopy glass full of holes, he was back to freezing, like on the heart-shaped island. But again, it was a strange time to feel nostalgic.

He was up this high just to get a quick glance at the floating harbor, to see exactly what they were up against, and do so before anyone down there knew he was looking in.

The monstrous floating complex was laid out like a huge T. The support ships were docked at the top; they doubled as its propulsion and support units, but for all the world looked like two gigantic apartment buildings looming over the docking area. A tall antenna was positioned between them; it was at least 500 feet high. A second, smaller mast was right beside it; Hunter was sure this served as an electronic jamming device. The six giant Ekranoplans were moored along the centerline of the T, three on each side, their snouts pointing inward.

That will help, Hunter thought.

He quickly turned back for the destroyer, now twenty-five miles to the west, and buried his throttle. They were doing the mission in complete radio silence, so it was important that he return to the warship at high speed.

Once there, he roared overhead and wagged his wings three times before circling back for a water landing.

This was code. Three times meant, "It's go-time . . ."

The destroyer spent the next hour heading west, battling the choppy seas at full speed ahead. The crew was called to battle stations. Gun teams reported to the ship's two main armaments: one twin-mounted three-inch Vickers gun up near the bow and another on the stern. Ammunition was brought up and the weapons were loaded.

The destroyer slowed only when the floating harbor showed up on its surface radar. They left the scope on for only a few moments—they didn't want to give away their position by presenting a hot radar dish. But they had it on long enough to confirm the floating base had a very large, military-strength communications antenna sticking out of a mast between the two supply ships. This tower was tall enough to send radio messages anywhere in the world. No doubt Viktoria's unhinged mother had been using it to harass her daughter from afar. And the jamming tower next to it all but ensured her abuse would go unanswered.

Running now on one-third power, the destroyer slowly approached the floating harbor, closing to within three miles of it.

So far, so good. The support ships tied to it were big enough to carry several hundred people, yet neither the destroyer nor Hunter had detected any defensive systems painting them on their approach. This was strange. The floating harbor was so out in the middle of nowhere, maybe its owners felt there wasn't anyone around to hide themselves from. Or maybe they were just stupid. Or arrogant.

Whatever the reason, this, too, would help the raiders.

The destroyer crept within 3,000 yards of the floating base and finally killed its engines. Captain Cheevers dared not get any closer.

Orr came up to the deck and focused his EAE super ears in the direction of the Ekranoplan base. It took him a few minutes to troll through the cacophony of voices before he finally heard one barking orders. He knew to key in on him because he sounded like a superior officer.

The information Orr got from listening to this booming voice was banal, but that's what they wanted. While he couldn't ascertain much about the Ekranoplan flight crews, he did learn that the crews of the support ships crews did a duty switch at 0200 hours or in about twenty minutes.

And that might bring activity on the docks.

Time to get to the next part of the plan—and quickly.

The destroyer launched two rubber boats. Oversized motors on both, thirteen people in each. Armed only with his Bowie knife, Hunter was in one; Orr in the other. Each boat also contained six volunteers from the destroyer's crew, each armed with an M-16. Filling out the raiding party were a dozen of Viktoria's *L'armee Bikini*, now wearing standard combat uniforms. They were led by the pirate queen's ski-masked security officer.

Each raft was also carrying a bag of gold coins.

They made their way over to the floating harbor, approaching carefully. But as before, they could see no security systems or even sentries anywhere on the monstrous platform.

Orr's boat reached the end of the dock first. They were at the bottom of the T with the six Ekranoplans right in front of them, docked on each side. They really were monsters up close; cruise liners with wings. The engine assembly was particularly odd: eight huge jet turbines positioned on a canard wing just a few feet back from the cockpit. The engine intakes were about ten feet up from the dock.

This was where Viktoria's pirates came in.

On arrival, the pirates broke into six pairs, each team carrying a rope and grappling hook. Moving like clockwork, they quickly reached their assigned Ekranoplans and used the rope to attach the grappling hook to the bottom of the huge vessel's engine assembly, all while being guarded by the armed Canadian sailors. Once the hook was secured, one pirate climbed up the rope and tossed a handful of gold coins into the front of each engine.

That's all they needed to do.

Hunter's team took the portside Ekranoplans; Orr's group took starboard. Hunter was impressed by how cool Viktoria's pirates were under pressure and how quietly they went about their business. They were amazing athletes and moved very gracefully back and forth in front of the massive engine columns.

Through it all, he could hear voices coming from the two docked supply ships. Many cabins had lights blazing within, as did their main bridges. Some guards could be seen walking the deck of the support ships, but still none were on the dock itself.

The whole operation took just five minutes. With both bags of gold expended, the raiders climbed back into their rubber boats and sped away, unseen, unheard, undetected.

That's when things started to go wrong.

In pure military parlance, what happened next was known as a cluster fuck.

It started with a great roar that rippled across the dark ocean. Both raiding parties heard it, even over the racket of their big outboard motors.

Hunter knew what was coming and turned back toward the floating base a few seconds before the shock wave hit. The base was suddenly lit up by dozens of searchlights; half were pointed straight up into the sky, the other half were trying to zero in on the escaping rubber boats.

In the next second a third bank of searchlights switched on, and they pointed due east. Coming out of their glare and the ocean mist was *another* Ekranoplan, this one with vivid red stripes painted on its tail section and fuselage. It was flying along on a cushion of air ten feet off the ocean's surface, slowing down as it was heading to dock at the floating station. Just one look at it in flight, though, and it was understandable why people called these things flying sea monsters. It didn't look like physics would allow it to do what it was doing—but here it was.

Then one of the docked Ekranoplans turned on its engines and the fistfuls of gold coins did their work.

Sucked into each engine's turbine fans, the pliable coins instantly disintegrated the spinning, high-speed blades, sending hot debris into the engines' combustion chambers, igniting hundreds of gallons of jet fuel pumped in for the start-up. Like eight little nuclear bombs going off at once, the Ekranoplan blew up in spectacular fashion, its forward section vaporized by the flames, its rear section doing a flip and coming down atop the Ekranoplan moored in the next berth over, blowing it up as well.

The resulting wall of flame roared high into the night. It was incredibly bright; it had to be visible hundreds of miles away. Hunter had never seen anything quite like it. None of them had.

The raging fire spread quickly to the other parts of the dock. Possibly in an effort to get away, another Ekranoplan started its engines. This caused an explosion as grand as the first two. The sky was lit up once again with a monstrous sheet of blue and orange flame. Hunter could feel the heat on his face, even though they were more than a mile away from the blasts.

But by this intense light, he could see that the red-striped Ekranoplan, arriving just as the fireworks went off, was now veering away from the burning harbor—and heading right for the two rubber boats.

No one had to yell any orders to increase speed. Both their motors were going full out, bouncing the rubber boats unmercifully atop the choppy waves.

But there was no way they could beat the sea monster.

It was getting closer and closer, like a jetliner crashing in a nightmare but able to stay aloft just ten feet off the water.

Its obvious intention was to swamp the rubber boats. Either the sheer dynamics of such a leviathan going over them would crush the inflatables or its jet exhaust would instantly melt them and catch them on fire. The disastrous results would be the same for those riding in the boats, and being thrown into the rough water would certainly finish the job.

Hunter looked over at Viktoria's masked security officer in the other boat, and each knew what the other was thinking.

"Split up!" they yelled in unison.

An instant later the rubber boats veered away from each other, though probably too late. Already the huge Ekranoplan vessel was almost on top of them, just seconds away.

But suddenly there were two explosions, both square on the monster's cockpit. The noise was deafening. The huge flying beast reacted by pulling up and toward the left. Its wing went right over Hunter's boat, pummeling it with backwash. But everyone hung on, and somehow they stayed out of the water. The other rubber boat survived as well.

Only then did they see a beautiful sight. It was the destroyer about a quarter mile away. Its forward deck gun had fired on the Ekranoplan's cockpit, killing its pilots and causing it to careen off at the last possible moment, sparing the rubber boats.

It all happened so fast, it took a few moments for the raiding party to realize that the *Shag Harbor* had just saved their lives.

Chapter Twenty-Four

The red-striped Ekranoplan was in trouble.

Its pilots were dead, its cockpit was on fire and the flying boat had hit the water extremely hard after taking two direct artillery hits on its nose. Violently spinning around on its left wing, it finally stopped moving after nearly a minute. But it was now dangerously close to sinking.

Its crew of twenty was frantically trying to do three things at once: keep the monster afloat, extinguish the cockpit fire, and, most important, protect the life of the very important person on board.

But while members of the VIP's personal guard ordered the crew to get life rafts ready immediately, there was a problem: The person they were protecting was . . . asleep. Despite being close to where three Ekranoplans just blew up, despite flying through some kind of battle, and despite the subsequent backbreaking hard landing on the ocean, she had slept through it all. And now none of her security detail wanted to wake her up.

The life rafts were readied, but at the same time, the fire in the cockpit had been put out and the crew had discharged ballast, righting the huge vessel.

Despite the thick smoke still wafting throughout its passageways, within five minutes of the hard landing, the pandemonium onboard the flying boat had died down. All vents and windows were opened, and the plane's air circulation system was put on emergency high. The vessel's redundant control system was turned on, and the flight engineers were slowly nursing the monster back to the wounded, heavily smoking floating harbor.

Only when the red-striped Ekranoplan had docked did the head matron enter the VIP cabin and gently rouse its occupant.

She was lying on her back, hands crossed over her chest like a vampire. Night mask on, a pistol close to her side, she was of undetermined age, but attractive. Jet-black hair, porcelain skin—and when she finally opened them, huge dark eyes.

She was Zvetlana Robotova, third wife of the world's worst villain, Viktor Robotov.

The matron greeted her softly, informing her that the Ekranoplan had arrived at its destination and reminding her that this was the time she'd left as a wake-up call.

The matron then exited the room; she would leave it to Zvetlana's security team to tell her what she'd just slept through.

*****

This they did, but only after she'd risen and had her morning cup of tea, sweetened with lemon vodka.

She took their news calmly, a fair surprise as she was prone to rages. She simply asked where the raiders were now and where they were believed to have come from.

The reply, stuttered into a few sentences by the nervous head of her security detail, was that they believed the raiders had come from a warship out of Foggy Bum Cay, their impending target. This warship was probably on its way back there now.

"Could you hit this vessel with our anti-ship missiles?" she asked, pouring herself another cup of tea. "Are they still functioning?"

"We believe they are," the man said. "On your orders we can employ our surface radar and hopefully pick them up. If we get a lock on the ship, we can try to sink it, out to a range of fifty miles."

"Then do it," she said simply.

The security men began to leave the cabin when she stopped them.

"This rough landing that I seemed to have slept through," she said. "Who was responsible for it?"

The chief security man was stumped for a reply.

Finally, he said: "That would be the pilots. They were both killed in the action."

She filled her cup a third time.

"Still, they failed me," she said coldly. "See that their bodies are cut up into chum and thrown to the fish. And make sure the next two pilots know in what condition their predecessors left this world."

Chapter Twenty-Five

Fifteen minutes later, Zvetlana walked into the damaged Ekranoplan's combat center, located right behind the damaged flight deck.

She was dressed all in black: a long gown split in the middle, knee-high leather boots, and a military-style jacket. She looked sexy, but in a disturbing way.

In that quarter hour, the crew had managed to turn the damaged flying boat around so its missile launchers were facing west. The vessel's sea surface radar screen took up one wall of the combat center. The system's operators had acquired a blip about 25 miles west of them; it was indicated by a red blinking dot on the big screen.

The operators told Zvetlana the blip might be the ship that had transported the raiders and fired on her plane's flight deck. It was the only vessel sailing within fifty miles of the still-smoldering floating harbor, though they couldn't be 100 percent sure it was the culprit.

Zvetlana waved away their concerns.

"Engage it," she told them.

The combat technicians took over, uploading the position of the red blinking light to the warheads of their first line of anti-ship weapons. Their launchers, three stacks that sat atop the rear section of the Ekranoplan's fuselage, carried P-280 Moskits. Somewhat similar to the Exocet missile, the P-280 flew just sixty feet off the water's surface and could carry a 600-pound warhead.

Get in the way of one and your sailing days were over.

Taking her seat—which was an elevated chair four feet higher than anything else in the war room—Zvetlana had some more morning tea and watched, via a TV screen, as the first three P-280s rocketed off their rails. There was a lot of fire and smoke at first, but when it cleared away, they could see three bright yellow lines on the radar screen heading for the blinking red light.

As soon as the missiles were in flight, Zvetlana told her intelligence officer to come forward.

She asked the man a question that sounded more like an afterthought.

"What are the chances my daughter is aboard that ship?"

The man almost stumbled on his reply. It was an impossible question to answer with any certainty. Zvetlana's naval force had been planning their attack on Foggy Bum Cay for two weeks. They were able to pick up some signal intelligence and knew approximately how many pirates were living on the island and where the center of their accursed fog-making machinery was located.

They also knew that Zvetlana's daughter Viktoria was the commanding officer of the pirate army and that she was most likely rattled after every one of her mother's taunting radio messages.

But whether she would have accompanied the raiders on their mission—that was hard to say. Viktoria was hands-on when it came to her operations, frequently leading boarding parties herself. Would she risk her life to go on the dangerous raid—and leave her troop leaderless if she did not return?

"Fifty-fifty, my lady," the intel man finally replied.

Zvetlana never took her eyes off the three yellow lines that were heading for the blinking red dot.

She sipped some more tea.

"Oh, well," she said with mock sincerity. "Too late now."

The missiles reached the target area one minute and ten seconds later.

Still represented by the yellow lines on the big radar screen, their color had intensified the closer they got to their objective.

"Twenty seconds to strike, Madam," the chief weapons officer told her. "All systems functioning."

But at that very moment, one of the bright yellow lines blinked out. One moment it was there, the next it was gone.

Zvetlana nearly came out of her seat.

"Why would that happen?" she asked loudly.

The board's techs went through a frenzy of switch-flicking and button-pushing, but nothing brought the missile's indicator back to life.

It was up to the chief weapons officer to give her the bad news.

"The missile might have malfunctioned," he said in a low voice.

Before she could react, a second missile indicator disappeared from the screen.

Now she was on her feet, getting as close to the big screen as possible. "Why would *that* happen?" she asked, voice raised.

More buttons pushed. Somewhere an alarm was going off.

As if on cue, the third light blinked out.

Suddenly the only light on the big board was the red one, indicating the destroyer was getting away.

Zvetlana turned on the weapons officer. The war room went silent.

"What are the chances all three missiles malfunctioned?" she asked him.

"Possible, but unlikely," he replied nervously.

"And what do you have as an alternative explanation?"

She actually took a step closer to the man. Just ten minutes before he'd been dragooned into the team that had to dismember the vessel pilots' bodies and throw them overboard to the fish. He didn't want to end up like that.

"They might have been shot down," he said finally.

"Shot down?" she roared. "How? By *anti*-anti-ship missiles? I don't recall anyone telling me that our missiles could be shot down this way. They move too fast."

The man gave a weak shrug. "Then it had to be an aircraft. Possibly an aircraft shot them down."

She came right up to him, face to face. Zvetlana was also known to hide an eight-inch switchblade in a sheath inside her right hip-high leather boot. Plus, she always carried her pistol.

"But such a feat, downing three supersonic missiles almost all at once, would take some extraordinary flight maneuvers, correct?"

"That's for certain," the weapons man said.

Zvetlana came up so close she was almost nose to nose with the trembling officer.

"Then let me ask you this," she seethed. "Who could possibly fly like that?"

*****

It was inaccurate to say that the Ekranoplan's missiles were shot down.

In the end, diverted was the better word. If you're crazy enough to fly across the flight path of a Russian missile with a 600-pound warhead going at supersonic speed, there was a possibility that your wash might disrupt the air current in front of it, screwing up the ram-jets at the last possible moment and causing it to crash, if you did it right. And if you were flying something faster than a prop-driven, fifty-five-year-old sea plane.

But that's what Hunter did.

They knew the anti-ship missiles would be coming, so the destroyer had a few minutes to prepare. Its crew practically threw Hunter's plane back into the water, the warship never really coming to a stop before hitting its engines again and taking off at high speed on a zig-zag course.

Meanwhile, Hunter got airborne quickly, nearly ripping the BB-4's engine off its top wing mount. As soon as he reached 1,000 feet, a climb that went nearly straight up, he leveled off—and saw below him the three red streaks of the P-280 missiles skimming along the surface of the water.

He knew at one mile out the missiles would go up to about seventy-five feet in altitude to maximize the blast of their huge warheads.

So when he saw the three missiles approaching, he did the math, figured out the best route to take, in the shortest distance and the shortest amount of time—and just did it.

Three times, in quick succession, he flew right through the P-280s' flight paths, disturbing the air flow in front of their ram jets, causing them to wobble and then nose dive.

That's how all three P-280s wound up getting splashed. He'd had such a small window of opportunity, in such a small amount of time, he just let his super-intuition take over and prayed the cosmos wasn't setting him up for a fall.

And it wasn't.

At least not this time.

Within three minutes of the P-280 missiles getting taken out, Hunter landed back beside the waiting destroyer and was quickly hauled aboard.

Once the destroyer was underway, Hunter went to the ship's communication hut, accompanied by Viktoria's masked security chief, who was looking no worse for wear after taking part in the floating harbor raid. After several tries, they were finally talking to the queen bee herself, straight from her second-story balcony.

It was a short conversation. Hunter did all the talking.

"You recall when we talked about Plan B?" he asked Viktoria.

"I do," she replied, not wanting to hear anymore. "We'll be prepared."

Hunter looked over at the masked security chief, who gave him a slow, almost sensuous thumbs up.

"And so will we," Hunter said. "But remember, they'll be right behind us."

Chapter Twenty-Six

Even another pot of sweetened tea could not contain Zvetlana's fury. And once unleashed, it was hard to put back in the bottle.

Enraged that her anti-ship missile attack failed at the very last moment, she gave a stunning order:

"Get underway immediately . . . full speed ahead. We are going after them!"

Her weapons officers were speechless. They knew this was not the thing to do.

"It would be prudent to wait until dawn, madam," the chief weapons man finally whispered to her. "We can re-supply the ship by then, fix what needs to be fixed, and perhaps take a few companies of soldiers with us. Plus, we can bring the other three Ekranoplans with us."

But she had her pistol out and in his mouth in a blink.

The man went pale.

"Are you refusing a direct order?" she asked, slowly twisting the gun barrel in the man's mouth.

The man was violently shaking his head no.

But she pulled the trigger anyway.

The weapons control crew rushed to their positions, trying their best to ignore the dying writhing officer as he was dragged away by some enlisted men. On the flight deck nearby, the Ekranoplan's backup pilots strapped into seats still covered with the blood of their fallen, fish-food colleagues. Temporary plates of cockpit glass were thrown into place, replacing those smashed to bits by the destroyer's twin blasts. But they were ill-fitting and made a tremendous noise once the monster started moving.

Nevertheless, the huge vessel was soon ten feet off the surface and traveling 250 knots, heading west, toward Foggy Bum Cay.

It arrived at its destination just before 4 a.m.

Shutting down its engines and lowering itself to the water's surface about a mile from the cay's lagoon, it commenced a murderous barrage of P-280 missiles. Fused for short-range flight, their anti-ship mission switched to land bombardment, all of them headed for the pirates' main base.

One P-280 would have done the job; two at the most. But by Zvetlana's orders, the volley lasted two minutes, eighteen missiles in all. Pathologically excessive, it vaporized the pirates' home, their headquarters, all of their fortifications, and a half mile of dense jungle in all directions.

When the missiles finally stopped falling, much of the island resembled a smoking moonscape. A small nuke couldn't have done a better job.

Shifting back into drive, the Ekranoplan, now moving as an ungainly conventional boat, maneuvered itself into the lagoon to examine what had been done. Nothing was left that they could see. The mangroves, the sea willows, all of the buildings were gone.

However . . . it was still very foggy.

Usually one of Zvetlana's Ekranoplans would carry two companies of marines, three hundred men in all, equipped with everything from heavy mortars to flamethrowers to small tanks.

But that was not the case here.

There was the Ekranoplan crew of twenty-two, counting the two substitute pilots. Zvetlana's security detachment numbered fourteen. Three dozen combatants, plus the Z-lady herself. Far below the usual numbers employed whenever she went out island shopping.

(That's exactly what she called it: shopping. Under her command, Zvetlana's monster force had taken over islands all along the European coast and throughout the Mediterranean. She would plunder the conquered isles and then hold them until someone literally bought them from her. Her biggest customer was the Russian NKVD, Moscow's most recent secret service and well known for its unparalleled cruelty. It was win-win for both sides—she collected booty and the NKVD added real estate and slave laborers for the expanding New Russian Empire. However, behind closed doors and away from any hidden microphones, people in the Kremlin often whispered that the whole thing—the troops, the Ekranoplans, the massive floating harbor—was set up by Zvetlana's husband just to give her something to do.)

Though under-manned and under-equipped, Zvetlana nevertheless ordered a landing party be dispatched to search the devastated island. Their orders were to find any survivors and execute them.

They wouldn't be gone long. Most of the island's surface had been wiped so clean there really was no place anyone could hide.

A landing party of three crewmen and three security guards launched off the Ekranoplan and paddled to shore.

It was just dawn and the sun's rays were trying very hard to pierce the especially thick fog around the lagoon. The landing party reached shore and beached their rubber boat. They waved to their comrades back on the Ekranoplan, anchored 200 feet away, and walked into the mist.

They were never seen again.

*****

It took a half hour of endless, one-sided radio calls and shouted meetings in Zvetlana's private cabin before a second team was assembled to go look for the landing party.

The sun was now up and getting hot. Calls back to the floating harbor told them that the other three Ekranoplans had not embarked yet. Their crews were moving as fast as they could to get underway, but they were still two or three hours away.

The rashness of Zvetlana's pursuit of the raiders was starting to come to light. Though she thought of it simply as beginning her planned invasion a little early, in any other situation, she would have been extremely vulnerable out here, alone in a vessel that was still smarting from some serious battle damage.

What bothered her crew the most, though, were their missing colleagues. There was no question that the Ekranoplan had leveled almost the entire cay. If nothing was left on the island, then what the hell happened to the landing party?

This answer became clearer just as the search party—all Ekranoplan crewmen—was climbing into their rubber raft. Suddenly the fog covering the lagoon blew away and many of those aboard the red-striped Ekranoplan realized that in the thick soup, three ordinary cargo ships had moved into position behind them, blocking their way out of the inlet.

The decks of these freighters were bristling with women and weapons. Behind them was a small navy of gunboats. And now, flying above, moving in and out of the fading mist, was a very strange little seaplane—with machine guns sticking out of its wings.

Seeing all this, the men of the second landing party simply raised their hands in surrender. Their comrades up on the flight deck did the same thing.

The Bikini Army had just captured an Ekranoplan sea monster without firing a shot.

The freighters maneuvered slightly to one side, allowing the gunboats to flood into the lagoon. Each one was carrying a dozen armed pirates.

As Hunter's BB-4 flew air cover low overhead, the gunboats quickly surrounded the sea beast. Armed with their grappling hooks and coils of rope, the pirates were soon swarming all over it, keeping the members of the aborted search party at bay and disarming them.

Completely unaware, Zvetlana was in her private cabin, brewing some more morning tea. She was upset that the landing party went missing, upset that she'd have to wait for the other Ekranoplans to arrive and then use their troops to scour the entire island looking for their missing crewmen. Making good of a bad situation, though, she decided to nap until her reinforcements arrived.

But then she heard a commotion outside her door. Shouting, banging, gunshots. People running up and down the passageway. She immediately pushed the red emergency button above her bed, summoning her security detail.

They usually appeared in seconds, but this time, no one came—and repeated attempts failed to bring them. What was going on? Had her bodyguards deserted her?

She took a huge gulp of tea right out of the pot and then retrieved her knife and pistol. She waited for her cabin door to open, not knowing what would be on the other side.

The noise in the passageway became louder. More footsteps, more gunshots, now some explosions. Finally, someone began banging on her cabin door. Zvetlana's first thought was one of relief. She was certain her security men had arrived at last.

But no.

Because when the door opened, for the first time in years, Zvetlana found herself looking into the gigantic dark eyes of her daughter, Viktoria.

Chapter Twenty-Seven

Ekranoplans 2, 4, and 5 finally got underway around 11 that morning, more than three hours late.

The delay had everything to do with what had happened the night before. Knowing now that their sea monsters had been sabotaged, each Ekranoplan needed all eight of its engines inspected and cleared of foreign objects. Then each vessel had to be fueled and armed, plus its company of marines and their equipment loaded on board. Finally, each had to steer its way out from the heavily damaged floating harbor before it could employ its air-cushion effect and truly get underway.

All this was not easy to do under the best conditions. It was especially tough with a third of the massive floating harbors either still aflame or smoldering. Just maneuvering the huge vessels around all the firefighting equipment and in the heavy smoke proved a huge endeavor.

Now acting on the barest of orders—the invasion of Foggy Bum Cay has begun early, get there as quickly as possible—the three huge flying boats finally cranked up their engines, lifted themselves up on their magic carpets, and headed west.

The communication units on each vessel spent most of the trip trying to raise Zvetlana's Ekranoplan, hoping to get a clarification of her commands. But none of them got a reply. They'd all received just that one and only radio message from her.

So it was with great surprise that, when they arrived at Foggy Bum Cay after thirty minutes of high-speed travel, they found the Z-Lady's Ekranoplan at rest about a thousand feet off the island's south coast, near the entrance to the big lagoon.

Flanking it were two dozen gunboats, three freighters, and a destroyer. A huge white flag sticking out of the red-striped Ekranoplan's damaged cockpit was billowing in the breeze. A small seaplane was flying circles overhead, looking down on everything.

The trio of sea monsters stopped at once, descended from their air cushions, and came to rest on the calm water just a few hundred feet away. Stationed three across, their crews were called to battle stations, but with strict orders to hold their fire. The commanders of the three vessels had no idea what was happening or what they should do.

It was then that their radios suddenly came alive. Plagued by static and slurred by booze, it was the unmistakable voice of Zvetlana.

"Comrades, our fortunes have turned against us," she told them. "But I assure you this is simply temporary. As you might have guessed, I am being held prisoner by our adversary. And they've asked me to send this message, to avoid further bloodshed, that you stand down immediately and return to our base."

The three Ekranoplan commanders were shocked. This was not the Z-Lady they knew.

After one long burst of static, she came back on. "But as soldiers," she said, quickly, "it's *your duty* to save me. So, *save me, you cowards*."

Then came the noise of a brief struggle . . . and then the line went dead.

But *that* was the Z-lady they knew.

It was not blind loyalty to Zvetlana that caused the commander of Ekranoplan 2 to launch his P-280 missiles.

It was pure fear of what Zvetlana would do to him if he didn't act. Plus, he'd convinced himself that once he fired his weapons, the adversary would recognize it as a show of force and back down.

But he was mistaken.

He launched three missiles; each was overshot. Instead of rocketing across the waves forty feet high, they went over at 100 feet, exploding on the far western end of the island, already flattened in the earlier bombard-ment.

Improper targeting, the heat of the moment—or maybe both. The volley proved more than useless. It proved deadly, because no sooner had the missiles landed when Ekranoplan 2 took a broadside from the *Shag Harbor's* pair of Vickers deck guns. At the same moment, every weapon on the pirates' gunboats opened up on the sea monster. There were armed people lining the decks of the freighters and they also unloaded on the flying boat, as did the circling seaplane, firing on the vessel's cockpit with its two wing-mounted machine guns.

Ekranoplans were not built for close-in combat. In reality, they were more like fast, heavily armed military ferries. They had little armor, and now it showed. The combined barrages sawed off the monster's tail section and severed its starboard wing. At least a dozen shells from the strafing sea plane perforated the flight deck. But when a missile fired by one of pirate gunboats hit the vessel's fuel tank, that was all she wrote.

The resulting explosion was so massive, it lifted the sea monster off the water, flipped it in mid-air and slammed it back down hard. The flying boat kept right on going, sinking in just a few seconds. There was some smoke, some bubbles, but then the waves covered over the mortally wounded beast and it was gone for good.

No sooner had the tremendous noise faded away when a communication link was reopened to the other two Ekranoplans.

It carried a different voice this time.

Younger. Stronger. Sober.

"This is Viktoria, daughter of Viktor Robotovich Robotov," the voice said. "And you would be wise to follow my orders from now on."

Chapter Twenty-Eight

The little universe around Foggy Bum Cay had changed forever.

The Bikini Army now had a real naval arm consisting of three Ekranoplans, each with three dozen P-280 missiles. It had also seized more than 200 of Zvetlana's fighters along with all their combat arms and ammunition. A real treasure chest of weaponry.

Once disarmed, the captured fighters were put in the hold of one Canadian freighter. The combined flight crews of the two remaining Ekranoplans were then installed on the ship's bridge. Given minimum provisions and some fuel, they were ordered to sail east and not come back.

Only one person from the Ekranoplan force would remain a prisoner.

Zvetlana.

The two other freighters were also made ready to sail; the *Shag Harbor* would escort them back to the real world, their crews unharmed, with an adventure for the ages.

Foggy Bum Cay had been nearly wiped clean. But the secret to the success of the Bikini Army was that they'd quickly transitioned into the vast underground chamber that served as the inner workings of the island's monstrous fog-producing mechanisms.

They would live down here, underground, at least until the island's vegetation grew back, which in this part of the world wouldn't take too long. Plus, it would be much cooler temperature-wise beneath the surface.

Already the pirates were discarding their brief swimwear for more typical attire like standard combat utilities.

Hunter had spent the next several hours trying to get the BB-4's radio to work, but with no luck. As far as he knew the Bikini Pirates had not touched it, as they had all the comm equipment on the Canadian vessels. It just seemed like the damn thing didn't want to work.

Around 3 p.m., he went to see Orr and the Canadians off. The *Shag Harbor* would at least partially complete its mission and escort two of the freighters back home.

Captain Cheevers offered to bring Hunter with them; all they had to do was hoist him and the BB-4 aboard. But he respectfully declined. He had to be sure that all of the hostages were truly free and a safe distance from Foggy Bum before he could even think about leaving. He and Orr exchanged contact information and he promised to reconnect as soon as he reached friendly environs. Then they said goodbye.

Sitting on the shore of the lagoon, Hunter watched as the three ships disappeared over the horizon.

He'd planned to spend that night underground himself.

The subterranean facility was essentially one huge open space, looking almost like a single floor of a vast parking garage. Doing double duty as pillars were the dozens of fog-generating machines. Actually little more than a collection of boilers, they created heavy, wet steam that was then blown through hundreds of vents via a massive fan and ducting system.

An adjacent underground section held a barracks and officers' quarters and it was here that Hunter had been given a small, single-room officer's billet.

It had a mattress, and by the time he finally called it a day, that was all he wanted.

But soon after he lay down and started to drift off to sleep, there was a knock at his door.

It was Viktoria's masked security officer. Once again, she pretended like Hunter wasn't there and did her job—making sure the space was secure. Confident it was, she motioned to someone in the hallway.

Viktoria walked in.

She was wearing a combat uniform similar to her security officer, but with four buttons undone from the top.

Her security officer slowly backed out the door and closed it, leaving them alone.

"I'm not sure of the correct American phrase for gratitude," Viktoria told Hunter, her voice heavy with emotion.

"Fulfilling your part of the bargain will be thanks enough," he replied trying not to stare at her unbuttoned buttons.

She looked around the drab little apartment.

"I'm sorry this isn't like the old place," she said with a sigh. "I mean, I'm glad we're all safe down here, and that I can keep an eye on the dragon-lady until I figure out a way to deal with her. But our old base had a certain charm to it."

"Just as long as I have a bunk, I'm cool," he told her.

She looked at him for a long time and then said: "Can you fly me somewhere? I have something I'd really like to show you."

Thirty minutes later, they were airborne in his little BB-4 seaplane.

It was cramped quarters; the cockpit was built for one pilot with a jump seat beside him. Viktoria was belted in, but with the constantly gyrating BB-4 and the hands-on flying it required, body contact was unavoidable.

They headed northwest. Night had fallen, the moon was just rising and the ocean was unusually calm. Viktoria talked almost the entire way—about her pirates, their adventures, herself. It was like they were on a date. And just like her masked security officer, the tight blue camo combat outfit definitely had a make-love-not-war look to it. She'd even brought a flask of rum with her.

They flew for about twenty minutes before coming upon yet another isolated mid-Atlantic island, this one just a blip on the map, unnamed, uncharted, but located very close to the apex of the Bermuda Triangle.

He set the plane down and they paddled it to a beach. The sand here was so fine and crystalline it glowed in the rising moonlight.

They climbed a pathway that led to a cliff overlooking the mirror-like Atlantic. The water was alive with phosphorescence, and moonlight lit the skies. They sat on an outcrop of rock at least 200 feet high and passed the flask of rum back and forth.

It was so strange, but Viktoria never really stopped talking. It was always interesting and oddly insightful, some of it even entertaining, though she said not a word about her family.

Omertà was obviously a tradition that did not end with World War III. But she was so unlike what he could ever have imagined Viktor's daughter would be.

She was in the middle of a story about taking over a ship that mysteriously had no crew aboard when she suddenly grabbed his wrist.

"Listen!" she whispered.

They fell still and he heard what must have been close to absolute quiet. No waves because the sea was so calm. No noise from the wind, because there was no wind. But she'd heard something. And a moment later, so did he.

A low drone, coming down from the north. Airplanes—he knew this right away. But not any kind that he'd ever encountered. He could tell just by the sound of the engines.

It took all of two minutes of hearing it before they finally saw it.

It was an enormous aircraft—bigger than anything Hunter could ever remember seeing. It was a bizarre design: eight engines, a twin tail, pontoons, and two extremely bright searchlights carried on its bottom at mid-fuselage.

It went right over their heads at not more than 3,000 feet high, looking to be just barely moving. Then, at the moment it passed over the tiny island, it made a long, slow bank to the east and flew in that direction until they couldn't see it anymore.

As soon as it disappeared, they spotted another giant aircraft approaching. It mimicked the first plane exactly, same direction, same altitude, same speed, same design. It, too, turned east at the same spot and vanished over on the horizon.

And another one followed after that, and then another, and another.

They sat there for nearly a half hour, watching the ghostly winged behemoths go overhead. They didn't look real to Hunter; they seemed more like holographic projections. But at the same time, they sounded very real. He was stunned, confused, and elated all at the same time and for a *long* time. He just couldn't take his eyes off them.

"They're out here every night," Viktoria told him as one of the last ones went overhead. "They're so strange, but beautiful, too. I'm assuming you've never seen that type of aircraft before?"

Hunter shook his head no, then added: "And I've been around."

"They always strike me as if they're looking for something," she said as the last one turned over their heads and faded off into the night. "The searchlights and all."

"Or they're lost," Hunter said. "And they're trying to find their way home."

She looked him in the eye.

"I don't mind telling you," she said, taking his hand again, "that I feel like I should be very conflicted at the moment. Growing up, my father hated you so much no one could speak your name to him. And if they did, they knew there would be dire consequences. But you just helped save my life, the lives of my fighters—and helped get my mother off my back. That's the biggest bonus of all."

She paused to take another hit of the rum.

"Strange things happen in this world," she went on. "We just saw one. But is it any stranger than you crashing on my island and walking into my court that day—of all days? I mean, really. What are the chances?"

Hunter just shrugged. "Sometimes I think most things are preordained by the universe," he told her. "No matter how crazy they seem, they happen because they were meant to happen from Day One. But other times, I swear all of reality is just chaos, and things are just colliding completely at random all the time. And every once in a while, something happens and it *seems* like it happened just for you."

She laughed in agreement. "You're right," she said. "There's no explaining it. Sometimes, things just happen."

Now it was his turn to look into her incredibly deep dark eyes.

"I can't be your friend," he said softly. "But I can't be your enemy, either."

She smiled, a little sadly. "I feel the same way," she said. Then she squeezed his hand. "But where does that leave us then?"

She pointed to the last of the huge ghost airplanes to fly over. "Searching for something? Or just lost?"

He took one more, long swig of rum and passed the rest to her.

"I just want to go home," he said, looking out on the sea. "Back to America. I'd swim if I had to."

She looked at him for a very long time. Those eyes of hers seemed to look right into his soul.

"Then you must go," she finally said, as if she'd solved some deep puzzle about him. "But not just because you fulfilled your part of the bargain. It's also because I think there's another damsel in distress out there who needs your help."

Chapter Twenty-Nine

The next morning, Hunter was back at the lagoon making a few final adjustments to the BB-4's engine. Fairly certain that all the Canadians were safe by now, it was time to leave.

He had about a half a tank of gas. His plan was to get back to Bermuda itself and then try to contact someone from there. If he had to land, he could tell them where to look for him—if his radio ever decided to work again that is.

After a few more engine adjustments, he was almost ready to go, though he was having a hard time believing it. Up until that moment, it all seemed like a dream to him. So much weird stuff had happened over the past few days, he'd started to wonder if this moment was ever going to come. But now that it was here, he wasn't going to waste time. That would be just like praying for something else bizarre to happen.

He finally strapped into BB-4's cockpit and prepared to start the engine.

"Just one more trip," he whispered to himself. "Just one more . . ."

Viktoria's empty rum bottle was still resting on the cockpit's jump seat, a reminder of their night together and their slightly drunken flight home.

As he was beginning his checklist, he noticed that a crowd of pirates had gathered on the small beach about fifty feet away. They were here to watch him go. It was almost a recreation of the scene not that long ago when the people of the heart-shaped island gathered to bid him goodbye.

He found himself scanning the growing crowd, looking for any sign of Viktoria—but she was not there. They'd parted with a very long embrace at the end of their adventure just a few hours before and came within a millimeter of a kiss, but did not.

He could still smell her perfume, though.

Sometimes, things just happen, he told himself.

He finished his checklist and finally started the cranky engine. It took a couple of tries, but it finally caught. He increased power and the engine began to roar. That was the sound he wanted to hear. He nudged the throttles ahead slowly but steadily. He just needed to see 6,000 RPM on his engine gauge, and for his two oil pressure lights to appear.

Once that happened, he would have to leave quickly. There was no fog, real or otherwise, about and the sky above was clear. But the lagoon was a tricky place to depart from because an ocean gale could blow in at any time, and it could be strong enough to ruin a perfectly good take-off. The wind was blowing his way at the moment. With no guarantees it would stay that way, he knew he had to get going now.

He looked over to the beach again to see about a hundred pirates had now gathered there, rum bottles in hand. It was a rowdy occasion, as it always seemed with them.

But still no Viktoria.

He was about to give them a salute and go when he saw someone waving to him from the beach, trying to get his attention.

No . . . it wasn't Viktoria wanting one last goodbye.

It was her masked security officer. She was holding Hunter's weapons—his trusty M-16 and his .357 Magnum.

He'd forgotten all about them. They'd been taken from him as soon as he surrendered, and he hadn't seen them since.

A small boat appeared and the security officer motored over to the seaplane. She climbed up the small access ladder and appeared outside his canopy door. Hunter lowered the window and gratefully took the weapons from her.

It was right at that moment that the engine reached the proper RPMs and his two oil indicator lights blinked on green. The wind was still right. It really was time to go.

He thanked her over the roar of the engine. Not only had she done a great job protecting her boss, she'd led the pirate contingent during the raid on the floating harbor, with spectacular results. She'd quietly been a big part of what had happened here since he'd arrived.

But when she lingered for a moment, he knew it was his only chance to find out just one more piece of information. He reduced his throttle a bit and cut down on the noise.

Then he asked her: "Do you ever take that mask off?"

It was strange, because it was almost as if she'd been expecting him to say just that.

"Are you sure you want me to?" she replied.

An odd question—he didn't know how to reply.

Finally, he just said, "Why not?"

So, in one fluid motion, she pulled the mask up and over her head, shook out her hair and slipped on a white baseball cap.

Then she just looked at him with a sly half smile.

Hunter's jaw dropped.

That face. Those eyes. The strawberry blonde hair.

It was the bargirl from the heart-shaped island.

"How?" was all he managed to sputter. "How . . ."

She just shrugged and gave him a full smile.

"Sometimes, things just happen," she said.

And that's how she left him. Pulling the mask back on, she retreated down to the boat and motored away.

Hunter wanted to call out to her, but a breeze against his face told him the ocean wind was changing, and if he wanted to get out of the lagoon, he had to go now.

He turned the seaplane 180 degrees, rumbled about 200 feet down the waterway, turned around again, and hit the throttle.

By the time he went by the beach again, he was traveling about 80 mph. The rowdy bunch of pirates were enthusiastically waving goodbye—but he saw no sign of the mysterious girl.

More baffled than ever, he was already well into his takeoff. He had no choice but to keep on going.

So he pulled back on the controls, goosed the throttle, and rose above the waters of the lagoon.

Then he slowly turned west, finally leaving Foggy Bum Cay behind.

PART THREE

Hamburg

Chapter Thirty

Not the least strange thing about Hunter's flight back was that as soon as the weird little island disappeared behind him, his radio suddenly crackled back to life.

One moment there was just the BB-4's engine and the loudest buzzing in his head he could ever remember—the next, an explosion of so many voices on the air, on every channel, he yanked the headphones off and pushed down the volume switch.

What the hell happened back there?

That question kept spinning around his head; *that's* what was causing all the buzz.

What the hell just happened?

The farther he flew, the more it really seemed like a dream. So when the radio came back, he was happy to pour all his energy into trying to get in touch with reality, or at least someone he knew.

It took about ten minutes, channel by channel, volume on 3, before he got through to a Free Canadian sea patrol plane flying off Cape Cod. They were a long way away, but they were able to patch him through to the USS *USA* on a scrambled line.

He spoke to Crunch for about ten minutes, trying his best to explain what had happened to him in the past few days. His good friend, extremely relieved to hear his voice, promised to get the word out that, yes, the Wingman was back from the dead . . . again.

After receiving a flash message that Hunter was safe, Fitz joined the radio conversation—but only for a few moments. He recited a set of coordinates, asked Hunter to fly to them, land, and wait for the next step. And then he was gone.

Hunter wanted nothing more than get back to the carrier, patch up his Su-34, and fly home. But he knew Fitz wouldn't have asked him to divert if it wasn't important.

He signed off with Crunch and started to search for the coordinates Fitz had laid out.

It took him a few minutes of consulting his maps and determining by the sun's position just where he was.

Again, his hope had been to make it to Bermuda, contact someone friendly, maybe get some gas, and then jump over to Norfolk, where he knew the USS *USA* would have docked to avoid the hurricane. Hearing from Fitz got his hopes up that his directions would bring him someplace civilized, taking out the guesswork.

But then he realized the coordinates actually put him almost at mid-ocean, two hundred miles from land, the closest being Walker's Cay, located at the very northern end of the Bahamian islands.

"Still inside the freaking Triangle," he groaned.

He arrived at the coordinates about ninety minutes later.

His calculations turned out to be all too correct. He was literally in the middle of nowhere. Again.

He put the BB-4 into a slow dive and circled down to where he was supposed to be. This part of his journey had been flown under radio silence. There was no one he could talk to about any of this.

He deployed his flaps and went skimming along the waves, finally settling with a great splash atop the ocean. It was still only eight in the morning and there was a sea mist at wave-top level. He never wanted to see fog again; he hoped the sun would burn it off quickly.

For some reason, he expected to be here a while. But as soon as his thoughts went back to Foggy Bum Cay and the strawberry blonde, he felt the airplane start to shake.

It quickly became violent, as if the ocean was rising up underneath him.

And that was not far from the truth.

Just 100 feet in front of him, the blue sea turned to black and the nose of a gigantic sea creature emerged from the depths. It caused a small tsunami that almost swamped the BB-4 for good.

When the seawater finally drained from his windshield, Hunter saw in front of him a gargantuan submarine. An Ohio-class Trident sub, to be exact. Nearly two football fields long, 18,000 tons, and a crew and passengers numbering 500. These things weren't just enormous, they were fast, silent, and could hide in the ocean for months—years, if need be.

This one happened to belong to his pal, Mike Fitzgerald.

Hunter was inside the USS *Fitz* ten minutes later.

He'd tied up to a ring on the port side of the sub, locked down the BB-4, and climbed aboard. Fitz met him at the top of the conning tower. They bro-hugged warmly, always glad to see each other.

But then Fitz hustled him down inside, indicating that they should not talk.

He led Hunter to his private cabin and opened the door.

"Someone needs to speak to you," Fitz told him.

Hunter walked in, Fitz slowly closing the door behind him. Sitting on a couch near the captain's desk was Hunter's longtime (and now ex) girlfriend, Dominique.

She was beautiful—more so every time he saw her. Regally appealing, long blonde hair, deep blue eyes, killer smile. Brigitte Bardot, for those keeping score. Wearing a plain long black gown, she oozed sensuality.

She rose off the couch and greeted him with a hug and a warm kiss on each cheek. Then she slapped him, somewhat gently. "You have to stop doing this," she scolded him. "Going missing all these times. Everyone was really worried."

"Sometimes, things just happen," he heard himself say.

She seemed reluctant to let him go. He looked into her eyes and realized she'd been crying. This was not good. They'd been through a lot together, and throughout she'd always been stronger than he. Tears meant something was wrong, something not trivial.

They sat on the couch.

"What is it?" he asked her. She was still holding his hands tightly.

"We know how Viktor escaped during the shipyard raid," she said, surprising him a little. "When he first built the place, he drilled a hole through the ice at the bottom of the harbor right underneath his berth. When the attack started, he released all that red smoke, submerged and got out that way."

"But how do you know this?"

She took a deep breath and replied: "Because Sergei found it out while on a mission in Russian Germany."

Sergei . . .

The name landed like a small bomb. Sergei Gagarin was a master spy. He'd played a key role in ending the Russian occupation of New York City, doing so while impersonating an army officer very high up in Moscow's food chain. That he'd fooled the Kremlin into thinking he was one of them was extraordinary, especially since Gagarin wasn't Russian at all. He was from Ireland, one of many Irish mercenaries who had helped Fitz and other freedom movements over the years.

But Gagarin was also Dominique's new significant other. They'd met in that strange period when she—and the rest of the world—thought Hunter was dead. Gagarin was dashing and handsome, and Dominique felt like a widow. And, well, sometimes, things just happen. Hunter still loved her very much and she loved him, but because of fate and time, both had moved on.

It still stung, though.

"Sergei sent back the information on Viktor's escape," she went on, "along with a lot of other things, like the fact that Viktor doesn't have any sun bombs left. They're all gone, blown up during your attack on *Sekret Ostrov*."

"That's excellent," Hunter said in small triumph. Viktor not having access to nuclear weapons was a good thing for planet Earth. "But how was Sergei able to get so deep inside Viktor's pants?"

"We don't know," she replied despondently. "We've lost contact with him."

She needed a moment to collect herself.

"After Sergei transmitted all that information, he was caught by the Russian secret police," she went on, her voice almost a whisper. She wiped her eyes again. "And now they're going to execute him."

Another small bomb. *This* was the crisis.

She collapsed in his arms—but oddly, he felt warm all over. He hadn't held her like this in a very long time, under any circumstances, so he gave himself a half second to enjoy it. Then he took her face in his hands and looked into her eyes. She was crying again—and he couldn't remember her looking so sad.

He tried to wipe away some of the tears but succeeded only in smearing her mascara. She was trying to say something, but couldn't.

It didn't matter. She didn't even have to ask.

"Don't worry," he told her. "I'll go get him."

Chapter Thirty-One

Hunter cleaned up, gulped down five cups of heavily sugared black coffee, and made his way to the sub's combat control center, better known as the C3.

It was a huge room for a sub, even something as large as the USS *Fitz*. It fit a conference room-size table, a dozen chairs, stacks of computers and communications gear, and because this was Fitz's boat, a fully stocked bar.

Fitz was in the room; so was Dominique, somewhat recovered, staying strong. Two of Fitz's operatives, agents Hunter knew only by their code names Trashman and Worm, were also on hand.

Hunter poured himself a sixth cup of coffee, loaded four spoons of sugar into it, and sat down. Fitz pushed a bottle of no-name whiskey in his direction.

"Add a splash, Mr. Wingman," he said in his thick Killarney brogue. "You're going to need it."

Attached to the wall just above the liquor cabinet was a large TV screen. Fitz pushed a button and it came alive with an old satellite photo showing a God's eye view of a very large harbor.

Hunter recognized it right away. Hamburg, Russian Germany.

"We're not sure how, but our friend Sergei has found himself here," Fitz said, using a laser pointer to indicate a red brick building on an island on one of the many tributaries that made up the intricate harbor. "It's an NKVD prison and detention center. Anyone the secret police believe is a threat to their occupation of the city, including their own soldiers, usually winds up here. But I think it's safe to say, Sergei is a special prisoner. That must have been a very secret Cookie jar he got caught rifling through."

He moved the pointer to another island, this one manmade and located about a mile north of the prison. It held a small airfield with a few buildings, an abbreviated runway, and a ski jump-style ramp, similar to those used on older Russian aircraft carriers.

But the tiny base looked abandoned.

"This was an airfield built specially for training in the naval Su-34s," Fitz told them. "Back when the Russians had some."

It was true. In the course of wresting New York City back from the Russians, the United Americans managed to capture dozens of the fighter-bombers. Officially, the seized airplanes now comprised a large portion of the United American Naval Air Force, the service that had conducted the Odessa Raid.

The photo of the tiny airfield told its own tale. There was no way an Su-34 or any other kind of fighter jet could operate from such a small airstrip without help. The ski jump allowed short, if sometimes hazardous, takeoffs. But Hunter also suspected the place was equipped with arresting wires, thick coils of steel that caught a landing jet by its tail hook, violently jerking it to a stop in a matter of seconds.

At Hunter's request, Fitz zoomed in on the runway. The closer he got, the more the arresting wires became visible, three in all.

"So basically, this place is the deck of a Russian air-craft carrier built on solid ground," Hunter said. "A place where rookie pilots could practice taking off and landing before going out to sea for the real thing."

Here were the beginnings of the rescue plan—Hunter could see it unfold before his eyes. Fly to Hamburg, land on one island, get to the other, spring Sergei, reverse direction, and get the hell out.

A simple plan—but with lots of unknowns.

"I wonder when's the last time those recovery wires worked," the Worm said.

Fitz just shrugged. "I'm sure they were oiled and greased this morning," he said dryly. "Same with that ramp."

He went back to the map. "They've got lots of SAMs scattered around the city. Lots of triple-A. This photo is about three months old and it came from one of the few spy satellites we still have access to these days. My guess is they brought even more SAMs in after we hit *Sekret Ostrov*. I'm hoping we can get a more up-to-date sat photo before jump-off, but that might not happen."

Hunter finally took Fitz's advice and added a splash of whiskey to his coffee. This just kept getting better and better.

Fitz tossed him the laser pointer. "Your thoughts, Hawker?"

Hunter took a gulp of the whiskey-laden, highly sweetened coffee.

"Flying in and out all depends on what it's like on the ground at that airfield," he began. "But let's say everything still works."

He pointed to the giant canal that separated the airfield island from the prison island. It was about a mile between them.

"That's pretty wide and it looks pretty deep," he went on. "And I'm guessing the current will be a problem. We're going to have to cross it in something motorized, especially on the way back."

He pointed to the prison building itself. Four stories, old, brick, drab. Maybe a warehouse in an earlier day.

"I'm sure there are guards down there," Hunter went on. "Just what else will we run into, though? Who knows?"

"We think he's being held in the basement," the Trashman said. "That would jibe with the NKVD's typical modus operandi."

It was at that one moment, and for the one and only time, that Dominique broke down just a bit. The mere mention of the NKVD was enough to do that to a lot of people. The Russian secret police were sadists when it came to interrogations, inhuman when it came to executions.

Fitz sipped his coffee and said: "We'll need a diversion, but I have some thoughts on that. If there's one thing we can do, it's make a lot of noise."

"And we've got to get in there when they least expect it," Hunter said, thinking out loud. "Like late Saturday night, when a lot of them will be drunk."

"But even before you talk attack times," the Worm said, "Isn't there the problem of crossing hundreds of miles of Russian airspace and so on?"

Hunter finished his coffee and poured another. He started the process of loading it up with sugar.

"Well, we'll be flying a Russian airplane," he said plainly. "We've just got to convince them that we're friends, not foes."

They hashed out dozens of details over the next few hours, trying to figure the logistics for such a mission and what kind of a diversion to cook up.

One thing was certain: The rescue party could ride in only one plane. Even if the recovery systems were still in place on the airfield island, there was no guarantee that their mechanisms were still working or that they could even handle a single recovery. Two was pushing it. Besides, plans thrown together last minute usually worked best if they stayed simple.

And this one was really thrown together.

But one plane didn't mean Hunter was going in alone. This was where the Su-34's Flying Winnebago design became a factor again.

This was going to be another really long mission. Under the best conditions, from their general vicinity of the mid-Atlantic to Hamburg was more than two thousand miles—one way.

They could get close to the European coast with the aid of buddy tankers, but after that, they'd be on their own. Fuel would be their most precious resource, especially if the diversionary plan worked anywhere near how it was supposed to.

Hunter was sure if they took out all the unnecessary stuff inside the Su-34, he could bring two men with him, and still have room for Sergei on the return trip. Six people flew off the heart-shaped island in the component plane they'd glued together. Carrying a maximum of four people shouldn't be a problem.

But who would go with him?

There were 500 people on the USS *Fitz*. About 150 of them were crew. The rest were mercenaries; one of the roles of the gigantic submarine was as a delivery truck for Fitz's private army. And among them always was a separate detachment of black ops personnel.

As it turned out, Hunter was friends with two members of the famous New York-based JAWS special ops team who were doing this tour with the Irishman. He'd known Jim Cook and Clancy Miller ever since the conclusion of the Third World War. Both had been instrumental in the recent victory over the Russians in New York. They were just the guys for the job.

Both men were brought up to the C3, listened to the mission stats, and immediately volunteered to go.

There was more coffee and one last quick chat with Fitz about the diversionary plan, then a silent, teary hug from Dominique. Then the three of them climbed out to discover the sub had arrived at its destination: a mid-sea rendezvous with the aircraft carrier USS *USA*. The boomer had made the entire trip on the surface after lashing Hunter's BB-4 to its deck.

It was the first time Hunter had seen the flattop so close from this angle: that is, sea level, looking up. It really was a colossus, a floating wall of steel that dwarfed Fitz's U-boat. Its hull alone blocked out nearly half the sky.

And as a testament to the ship's engineers, they'd finally gotten the carrier's engines running on their own, so there was no longer a need for the small navy of tugboats pushing and pulling it everywhere. Those engines were put to the test early as they had steamed at full power to reach the mid-ocean meeting point.

The carrier's crew had already retrieved the BB-4 seaplane. Hunter and the two JAWS troopers transferred to the carrier via a launch and climbed up to the flight deck. A swarm of aircraft techs was already working on Hunter's Su-34, adapting it for the mission ahead after earlier fixing as many dings as they could resulting from the Odessa Raid and his subsequent adventure on the heart-shaped island.

It was now mid-afternoon in the mid-Atlantic. Hunter looked over the side and saw Fitz and Dominique standing out on the conning tower's porch. Seeing the Wingman and the two troopers were safely on board, Fitz called out an order, gave Hunter a quick salute, and disappeared back into the sub.

That left Dominique alone for a moment. Her blonde hair blowing in the ocean breeze, she looked up at him, touched her heart twice, and disappeared.

Its tower hatches secured, the water under the *Fitz* began trembling fiercely. Then the giant sub started going down, slowly slipping below the waves.

A few seconds later, Hunter couldn't see it at all.

Chapter Thirty-Two

The local German population called the building on the canal island *Das Blutgefangnis*.

The Blood Prison.

A sign on its boat landing said it all: *Nur wenige, die reinkommen, kommen heraus.*

Few who go in ever come out.

The place was run by the NKVD, the Kremlin's vile secret police. There were 30,000 Russian occupation troops in Hamburg along with two million civilians. The troops lived downtown in a military restricted area, off limits to anyone who wasn't Russian. These troops always had the NKVD looking over their shoulders, though, listening for the slightest hint of disloyalty to Moscow. Offenders were dealt with swiftly.

This was one benefit for civilians not being able to enter the city proper: They could usually steer clear of *Das Blutgefangnis*.

The island itself was a perfect square, 500 feet on each side, built on a pier of steel pilings and red bricks. The prison held four stories above ground, a vast cellar below, but very few jail cells. They were rarely needed.

The enormous basement was its interrogation center. Fitz's intel guys believed it was laid out like a maze, with seemingly endless, overlapping, dimly lit corridors designed to emphasize the horror of the place. For anyone unlucky enough to be brought here, the message was clear: once in, there really was no way out.

There were a dozen grilling rooms, though they looked more like showers, as each had a drain in the middle. After particularly gruesome questionings, blood and bodily fluids could be washed away. Still, the people who worked upstairs in the prison frequently complained to Moscow that the cellar smelled like a meat-packing plant. This only added to its infamy.

At the center of the labyrinth was a room containing the NKVD interrogators' collection of torture devices. Hand-cranked electrical generators, rolls of piano wire, tire irons, razors, dental pliers, bone-slicing hand saws— and their most hideous tool of all, lidocaine.

The NKVD inquisitors would torture someone to the point of death, only to have an NKVD physician inject lidocaine directly into the victim's heart, literally bringing him back to life to be tortured further. This could go on for hours, even days—the victim begging to die, only to be denied over and over by the sadistic executioners. Only when they grew bored with the sport would the torturers fire a bullet into the victim's throat and watch him drown in his own blood.

Sergei Gagarin was an unusual inmate for *Das Blutgefangnis,* though.

He was not a disloyal, loud-mouthed Russian soldier. He was a master spy who was caught rifling through files inside the Russian military headquarters on the Floggen-bahm by a civilian painter who'd forgotten his brushes. This man spread the alarm only because had he chose not to, it would probably have meant his own life and those of his family.

The NKVD determined Gagarin had penetrated the Russian High Command a week before, impersonating an army liaison officer from Moscow whose murdered body was later found in a Hamburg brothel. The secret police determined Gagarin had already sent troves of classified information to whomever he was working for, most likely the United Americans, the same people who'd bombed *Sekret Ostrov*, Viktor's top-secret Arctic headquarters, just two weeks before.

When Gagarin refused to talk, the NKVD put elec-trical cables on his genitals and hung him from a meat hook for hours at a time, sending massive shocks through his scrotum while his toes hovered just an inch above the floor. They also put piano wire around his neck and tightened it until he could hardly breathe and took turns beating him with tire irons and truncheons.

Coming close to the edge of death many times, Gagarin was injected with huge doses of lidocaine by the prison's doctor. It served to keep the spy wide awake and breathing and hyper aware of what was happening to him.

But all this was soon to end.

This unusual visitor had not talked in five days and, by now, probably wasn't able to. The NKVD was through dealing with him.

Tonight would be his last.

The sun went down and the lights came on in downtown Hamburg, the only part of the city where electricity use was allowed at night.

Many off-duty Russian soldiers headed for the bars along the Repperbahn, a few blocks from the docks, intent on getting drunk and laid. By all indications, it would be a typical Saturday night in Occupied Germany's second-largest city.

But all that ended shortly before 8p.m. Just minutes after the sun went down, the early evening was split by the wail of sirens. Unknown aerial targets were approaching Hamburg from the west. Searchlights lit up the sky. The city went into mandatory blackout. Russian anti-aircraft crews—many towing SAM missile launchers; others pulling triple-barrel AA guns—were soon racing through the streets.

At the same time, fighter aircraft began scrambling from the now-militarized Hamburg International Airport. In just a few minutes, the skies above the city were crowded with Russian fighters, many of them ground-based versions of the Su-34.

Hamburg was about to experience its first air raid in decades.

A swarm of cruise missiles arrived over the city at exactly 8:10 p.m.

They came in three waves, tripping every anti-aircraft radar in the occupied zone. Suddenly all of the Russian military's communications centers went off the air, disrupting the stream of highly centralized orders to Hamburg's defense forces.

But this only lasted for a few seconds.

When communications were restored, the defense forces heard Russian voices almost indistinguishable from those before, barking out new commands. Pilots in flight were ordered not to shoot at the incoming cruise missiles; they should hold their fire for battle against the formation of enemy attack planes the radar said were following close behind. The Russian fighter crews were told the approaching air raid was going to be a carbon copy of the recent attack on *Sekret Ostrov,* and that the same tactics were being used. First cruise missiles, then an aerial bombardment by jet aircraft.

But orders received by Russian anti-aircraft units on the ground told them something completely different. Stating that *no* Russian fighters had launched yet and that intelligence reports indicated the impending air raid was being conducted by United American pilots using captured Russian planes, the anti-aircraft crews were told to shoot at anything they saw flying over the city.

This led to utter confusion. As the AA teams opened up on their own fighter planes, the Russian fighter pilots watched helplessly as the swarm of cruise missiles went by them and started plunging onto the city below.

In minutes it was an *enormes Clusterficken*—no translation required.

The first wave of Tomahawk cruise missiles hit Hamburg's west side docks, home to a massive fuel farm and tanker loading facilities. Five gigantic explosions rocked the area, igniting dozens of oil tanks. In seconds, flames reaching hundreds of feet in the air lit up the night sky.

A second spread of missiles hit the Hamburg airport, destroying the control tower, cratering its main runways, and wiping out all of the city's military communication and command centers. Now those Russian fighter aircraft circling their way through the crowded, dangerous skies above Hamburg would have to find somewhere else to land after doing battle with the incoming enemy airplanes. Or when their fuel ran out.

The third wave of Tomahawks hit the entrance to Hamburg's *Nikolaifleet,* the largest canal in a city of canals. It unleashed a tidal wave of water that raced through the streets of downtown, causing damage rivaling the two previous cruise missile barrages.

This was the scene at twenty minutes past 8 p.m. Russian fighters continued to circle the city, trying to avoid being shot down by their own AA units, those same AA units firing on the fighter jets because they thought they're being flown by Americans.

Meanwhile, large fires swept the oil docks and the airport was no more.

About the only place in Hamburg not caught up in the bedlam was the dungeon at *Das Blutgefangnis.*

Its torture chambers were heavily sound-proofed, so its victims' screams could not be heard upstairs or beyond the building's outer walls. But the exterior sound-proofing worked both ways. It was so good, those down inside this dreadful netherworld were oblivious to what was happening outside.

In Interrogation Room #3, three men were now taking turns beating Sergei Gagarin. He was laid out on the floor this time, spread-eagle, face up, his arms and legs bound with rope tied to eye hooks in the walls. Two of the men were using their hobnail boots to stomp his extremities. The third man was systematically working him over with a tire iron: shoulders, elbows, knees, feet, repeat. A fourth man was on hand. Standing in the corner, calmly smoking a cigarette, he was watching the others pummel the prisoner to death. He had a body bag unfolded and ready nearby.

After one gruesome blow to his head via a tire iron, the prisoner vomited a stream of blood and then became motionless. The end seemed near. But the interrogators had not yet grown bored. So they signaled the fourth man to come forward.

He was an NKVD doctor. He took out a giant syringe, wiped the blood from the man's chest, and injected him with twenty ccs of lidocaine directly into the heart.

Gagarin's limp body suddenly came back to life; it happened so quickly it was as if he raised right off the floor, lifted by unseen hands. The three other men resumed battering him. Two minutes into this assault,

Gagarin collapsed to the bloody floor again, let out one last gasp for air, and fell still.

The doctor came forward and once more brought Gagarin back to life, this time with forty ccs of lidocaine. But he was nearing the end of his supply.

He told the interrogators: "I've got three shots left. If you need more than that, I'll have to get another vial."

One of the men waved him off. "Not necessary," he said, throwing away his bloody tire iron. "If he hasn't talked yet, he never will. Plus, I'm hungry."

There was a brief discussion about who would deliver the coup de grace. The most veteran man in the group was finally designated executioner. He took out his Makarov pistol, lifted the man's head from the floor, and put the barrel directly onto his Adam's apple.

The others laughed.

"Pull and let's eat," one urged the man.

Getting out of the way of the coming blood splatter, the man started to squeeze his trigger when he suddenly felt a strange warmth filling his body. He looked down at his chest to see a hole the size of his fist just below his ribcage. It was spurting blood like a fire hose.

He said one last word: "How?"

Then he fell over dead.

The other interrogators were stunned. They looked behind them to see the door to the room was open and three Russian pilots were standing there, wearing over-sized helmets with dark visors hiding their faces. They seemed frozen in place as if they, too, were having trouble understanding exactly what was happening.

"Who are you?" one man shouted at them in Russian.

"How did the air force get in here?" another asked.

They never got their answers. Each man standing in the doorway fired a single round from his M-16. Three tap shots, each to the skull, and the interrogators and the doctor joined their friend in hell.

Only then did Hunter, Cook and Miller take off their helmets.

They knelt around the dying spy, nearly without words. Blood was oozing out of him from so many places, they dared not touch him for fear anywhere they put their hands would cause him intense pain.

"Wow—what a mess," Cook finally blurted out.

"We're too late," Miller added; he was the medic of the group. "Look at him. There's no way we can move him without killing him."

Hunter put his head in his hands. They'd tried to plan for every contingency in the hastily assembled rescue mission.

"But we sure didn't think of this," he whispered.

Getting to Hamburg had taken split-second timing, some crazy flying, and a lot of blind faith that the cosmos would somehow look out for them.

As soon as the USS *Fitz* dropped them off, the giant sub had raced to a location close to the island of Guernsey, south of the British Isles. Hunter, Miller and Cook launched from the USS *USA* just before sunset, followed by a Su-34 buddy tanker flown by Ben Wa and JT Twomey. Both planes had been hurriedly repainted from blue to black, with their U.S. emblems removed and replaced with the Russian red star. Adding to the charade, Hunter and the two JAWS operatives were wearing what they hoped would pass for Russian air force flight suits. This, of course, would make them saboteurs, and if caught they would be shot on the spot.

Once airborne, they turned northeast, their nose pointed toward Occupied Germany. They did a nail-biting aerial refueling with Ben and JT off the French coast in bad weather. Then tanks topped off with gas, Hunter put the big Su-34 down to an earth-scraping fifty feet and, hoping to stay under the Russian radar, hit the afterburner and headed inland.

Meanwhile Ben and JT went into a long wide orbit off Normandy and waited.

At precisely 7:45p.m., the USS *Fitz* launched the three waves of Tomahawk cruise missiles from its position off the Channel Islands. Their target: downtown Hamburg. At that same moment, two of Fitz's agents working inside the city switched on a portable ECM radio-jamming pod and blacked out the entire Russian communications net, but only for a few seconds before broadcasting a previously taped set of false orders to the Russian pilots and anti-aircraft crews.

Hunter's aircraft was twenty miles from Hamburg when the first cruise missiles hit. He, Cook, and Miller could see the explosions all around the center of the port city and watched as Russian searchlights madly tried to lock onto the modern-day V-1s buzzing overhead.

As diversionary tactics go, it was spectacular.

Exactly sixty seconds after the first cruise missile detonated, Hunter pulled back on his controls and soared to 20,000 feet. Within a minute, they'd joined the carousel of Russian fighters circling above the burning city, just one of two dozen Su-34s dodging AA fire, still awaiting the massive air assault.

Once Hunter saw he was over the city's docks, he simply dropped out of the merry-go-round, went back down to fifty feet and reduced his speed to a 110-mph crawl. He flew down the flooded Repperbahn, weaving his way in between the skyscrapers before finally turning east onto the Kraftwerk Canal.

Spotting the island airfield, he told Cook and Miller to hang on and then lowered his landing gear. Two seconds later they slammed down on to the island's sole runway, the Su-34's tail hook just barely catching the only arresting cable still working at the abandoned base.

It was like landing in the middle of hell. Both sides of the Kraftwerk Canal were on fire. Buildings, docks, oil tanks. The smoke was thick, and flames billowed everywhere. The noise alone was tremendous. But though their arrival was more controlled crash than a landing, they were down, still intact, and, as far as they knew, no one had noticed.

Hunter scrambled out of the plane and ran to the end of the runway. He had to check the island's takeoff ramp. If it wasn't functional, they would be royally screwed. At the very least, it would be a long swim home.

He reached the ramp and gave it a quick once-over with his NVGs. He wished it was perfectly intact, but it wasn't. Some of the outer planks were burned and others were smoldering. The whole thing looked creaky to begin with.

But could it handle one more takeoff?

He couldn't tell.

He ran back to the Su-34 and re-joined Cook and Miller. There was so much pandemonium around them, Hunter was almost certain if anyone had spotted them, they would just assume they were a Russian crew making an emergency landing because Hamburg airport was out of commission. Or at least, that was part of the plan.

They quickly inflated their tiny raft and hooked up the small electric motor. Then they set out on the Kraftwerk Canal, heading toward *Das Blutgefangnis,* one mile away.

It was not a smooth voyage. The city was now being bombarded by a fourth wave of Fitz's cruise missiles—some of them were flying right over their heads. But they were doing their job almost too well.

Destroying the *Nikolaifleet* and flooding the downtown had conspired to create a mammoth tide in the Kraftwerk Canal. The wreckage from so many exploding buildings collapsing into the waterway had created waves higher than six feet—and they were hitting the raft from every direction. Even worse, flaming debris from falling aircraft, SAM missile casings, and expended anti-aircraft shells was coming down all around them. One unlucky hit on the raft and the game would be over for them.

They were almost swamped numerous times during the one-mile dash, but they made it somehow, Hunter sending a quick thank you to the universe for that.

Tying up at the prison island's main dock, the plan was not to hide or skulk around; rather, they would rely on their grand entrance and their Russian air force uniforms to keep up the pretense long enough to overwhelm anyone who got in their way.

But it made no difference. There were no guards watching the front door of the blood prison. They'd either fled or sought shelter inside. The building was dark with no emergency lighting, no signs of life at all. Nevertheless, Hunter and the two JAWS officers went through a window in the back and followed signs leading to the Interrogation Section.

Down two sets of stairs, they were quickly inside the basement dungeon. That's when they realized their intelligence report was a bit off when it said the place was a maze. It was more like an Escher drawing. Some hallways ended for no reason; others crossed each other at weird, nonsensical points. Twice they were faced with three different corridors to take—and all three times wound up back where they started. Dark and clammy, it was also filled with bizarre noises including the sound of children screaming and women crying, all piped in over hidden speakers.

Despite all this, after just five minutes of searching, they'd found the right interrogation room simply by following the unmistakable sounds of someone being beaten to death.

That had been three minutes ago.

And while the most immediate threat had been eliminated by their M-16s, they knew the building's guards were probably down here somewhere, along with more sicko interrogators.

But Gagarin's condition was far worse than they could have imagined. As the team's medic, Miller had anticipated some injuries.

But nothing like this.

He put his ear to Gagarin's chest and just shook his head.

"He's checking out," he said forlornly. "I can't believe he's still breathing."

Cook turned to Hunter. "What are we going to do, Hawk? Fitz's show is going to end soon. When these morons realize they've been duped, they'll be very unhappy with us."

Hunter started running through the options in his head, but it didn't take very long. Their choices were limited. There didn't seem to be a place on Gagarin's body that wasn't broken or bleeding. And having just made the perilous trip over from the airfield to the prison, they couldn't imagine how they could get the spy back to the airfield in the raft without killing him themselves.

Miller checked Gagarin's pulse again. It took him a long half minute to find one, finally, on the spy's broken right wrist. But it was barely there.

Miller looked up at Hunter. "Should we just wait?" he asked. "It won't be longer than a few minutes."

Hunter's head started to do a slow spin. He knew what Miller meant. Moving a dead body was a lot easier than one that was still breathing, especially when almost any movement could hasten the end.

But Hunter just couldn't do it.

Not to Gagarin.

Not to Dominique.

That's when he turned his attention to the dead man in the corner.

There were syringes and needles littering the floor around his body. Hunter picked up one of the used needles and rubbed it against the fingers of his glove. Then he put his fingers to his tongue.

"Lidocaine."

It had an unmistakable taste.

"I can smell it from here," Miller said.

Hunter gathered up the man's medical bag.

"Screw it," he said. "Let's wrap him up and get back to the plane. If we kill him, this stuff will help us bring him back."

But now they had to get out of the maze.

As they were running full out toward the sounds of Gagarin getting beaten to death, Hunter had tried to make a mental map of how they finally arrived at the correct interrogation room. Right, left, left, two quick rights and another left and there they were at Door #3.

But now he had to recreate that route exactly . . . in reverse order.

With Cook and Miller carrying Gagarin in the NKVD's body bag, Hunter went out of the room first and took a right. They had removed their flight jackets and did their best to bundle them around Gagarin, if just to stop the flow of blood—but they instantly became soaked in it instead.

At the end of the first darkened hallway, Hunter took them right, bringing them into another long, dimly lit corridor.

This looks familiar, he thought.

But then again, that was the whole idea behind a maze. It all looked familiar . . . until it didn't.

More running, Hunter with his M-16 out in front, Cook and Miller doing their best to keep up behind him.

Another junction of hallways. Hunter turned them right again.

Yes, he remembered this. So far, so good.

But just a second later, all three came to a skidding halt.

Voices . . .

Behind them. In front of them. Both right and left.

Men shouting in Russian. Men responding to orders. Then footsteps. Lots of them.

Their black ops experience told Hunter and the two JAWS officers to stay frozen just long enough to get a location point and a count, and then prudently head off in the other direction.

But that was the problem.

The voices were coming from all around them.

Not good.

They started running forward again, but suddenly the hallway became seeped in a low fog. And they seemed to be descending, going farther down into the basement dungeon, not upward and out of it as they needed to be.

Another junction of hallways; they went left, then left again—but this brought them to a short corridor and beyond was a convergence of *five* hallways.

None of this looked familiar.

They could hear more people running toward them, more voices shouting. And then gunshots.

But which way to go?

Hunter told the others to lie low for a moment. Miller took the time to inject the lifeless Gagarin with a syringe full of lidocaine, the first of three shots remaining. The spy's body jumped, and he began softly gasping for breath. He was still alive, but barely.

Meanwhile, Hunter started off through the fog, down the short hallway to the conjunction of five passageways, hoping that he could figure out, very quickly, which way to go. In those few seconds, they all lost sight of each other.

He reached the junction and came to another stop, his flight boots sliding on the slimy floor. Each of the five hallways looked the same—and all of them looked to be headed downward.

They certainly hadn't passed this way running in. And now he was faced with five choices on which way to get out—six if he counted the option of simply reversing themselves and running in the opposite direction.

He begged his ESP gift to show him the way, but nothing seemed to be working.

Until . . .

He suddenly realized someone was standing in the mist right next to him. Wearing a long black cloak and hood, they looked like something from a ghost movie.

The figure was pointing to the middle hallway. A female's voice coming from under the hood whispered urgently to him: "That way. Go—that way."

It was one of those times in Hunter's life when everything just came to a halt.

Cook and Miller were behind him somewhere. He could still hear voices shouting, and gunshots pinging off walls nearby. The fog was building, and if anything, the lights were getting dimmer.

But this he had to know.

"Who are you?" he asked her.

She pulled back the hood just enough to reveal her face. She looked at him—and smiled.

But what was really strange was he didn't recognize her—at first. So she pulled the hood all the way back to reveal that she was wearing a white baseball cap underneath.

That's when it hit him.

It was her. The girl from the bar on the heart-shaped island. The one under the mask back on Foggy Bum Cay.

He went numb, head to toes. Weird things had happened to him his whole life, but nothing even close to this.

She just shook her head, strawberry blonde curls swaying this way and that, and laughed at his reaction.

"Are you . . . an angel or something?" he heard himself say.

She gave him that look and said: "Do you really want to know?"

But she didn't wait for him to reply.

She commanded him: "Get your friends and go! Take the middle hallway—hurry!"

Hunter half-ran, half stumbled back up the hallway, collected Cook and Miller and Gagarin's limp body, and ran back down to the convergence of hallways.

But by then, the girl was gone.

Chapter Thirty-Three

The middle hallway led directly to the front door of the prison.

It was unguarded just as before, but Hunter, Cook, and Miller could still hear footsteps behind them, people chasing them in hot pursuit.

They stumbled out of the prison to find the conflagrations lit off by Fitz's cruise missiles had joined together to become a firestorm, gigantic and out of control. They could hear the siren wails of the *feuerwehrautos* screaming through the streets on their way to battle thousands of fires. The entire military zone in downtown Hamburg looked ablaze, the wind whipping flames into dozens of miniature tornados. The heat was searing. The air thick with smoke.

But they had to stop. Miller had been trying to get a pulse on Gagarin even as they were running along the last hallway, but could not find even a blip.

"So we killed him?" Cook asked sadly.

Miller replied: "Maybe not yet."

He refilled his syringe with lidocaine and jammed it into Gagarin's heart.

The master spy came alive again—and for a few seconds, it appeared as if he knew what was going on. He stared up at them and realized he wasn't looking into the eyes of the most despicable people imaginable anymore. These were his friends. Then he glanced down at his battered body and saw he was being carried in a body bag and that he was actually outside the blood prison—and started to cry.

He grabbed Hunter's arm with near-superhuman strength.

"Don't be fools," he whispered weakly in a thick Irish brogue. "I thank you for trying, lads, but please go. Please save yourselves . . ."

This knocked Hunter out of his stupor caused by what had just happened back in the maze. For the first time in a long time, he smiled. He couldn't help it.

"You've got to be kidding," he told the master spy.

Gagarin started to laugh, but then his eyes rolled back into his head, he coughed up a mouthful of blood and lapsed back into unconsciousness.

So much for that . . .

They picked up the injured spy again and made for the island's small dock.

While it was no surprise that the chaos outside had grown worse, it was a shock to see the Kraftwerk Canal itself was on fire. So much flaming debris had fallen into it, the oily surface had ignited into a literal sea of flames.

Their little motorized raft was still there, but the heat was so intense it was melting before their eyes. It looked about two-thirds its original size and was still shrinking.

But there was no other way to go. They carefully lifted Gagarin into the hot, smelly raft, laying him on the bottom where the water began seeping into his wounds, making everything sticky and bloody.

The raft's motor didn't start, again no surprise. Hunter heaved it overboard and they began paddling with their rifle butts.

They were going with the current this time, but the canal was now like a flaming, floating obstacle course. Entire sections of buildings blown apart, large jagged pieces of expended SAM missiles, wrecks of cars and trucks swept away by the giant flood from the bombed Nikolaifleet Canal. Half of them were still on fire. They did their best to maneuver around all of it with their gun-stock paddles, at the same time trying to keep the raft under control in the swift current.

And it worked, until about halfway to the airfield island.

Then disaster struck.

A Russian jet fighter, shot down by its own troops, came out of the sky in a massive fireball and crashed into the canal not 200 feet away from them. The plane sank immediately, but the wave it created hit them a few seconds later—and next thing Hunter knew, he was underwater, tangled up in the overturned raft's tow rope.

He spent ten long seconds fighting not to be pulled to the bottom with the suddenly deflated, rapidly sinking raft. Only because he was able to get his knife out quickly and cut himself free did he not go down with it.

When he finally broke through to the surface, he found Cook was holding up Gagarin, and Miller was holding up Cook. He swam over to them and, with great effort, they lifted the spy out of the water just enough so Hunter could tie his utility belt under the dying man's arms.

Now able to swim on their own, Miller and Cook created a human chain. Hunter put the end of the utility belt in his mouth. Then Cook started pulling Miller, who in turn was pulling Hunter who was pulling Gagarin.

It was incredibly awkward and difficult, but thanks to the fast current, they began moving again toward the airfield island.

It took another twenty minutes to go the half-mile distance, all the while the fires were increasing all around them, flaming debris was falling everywhere and the tremendous heat was rising by the second.

Many tormenting thoughts went through Hunter's mind during this long swim. Would the Su-34's engines start? Had the plane itself been spared in the thunderstorm of falling debris? How about the wooden ramp? Was it still intact?

Gagarin felt like such dead weight during the arduous journey, Hunter was sure the spy had finally given up the ghost. How would he break that news to Dominique? And how badly would the United American cause be affected by the loss of an intelligence genius like Gagarin?

But with all this swirling around in his mind at supersonic speed, he still kept coming back to the same thing.

Who in God's name was the girl in the tunnel?

The three of them were beyond exhaustion when they finally reached the airfield island. They were covered with oil and blood, soaked through with the putrid canal water, and it took a major effort just to crawl up onto the small beach, dragging Gagarin behind them.

Hunter put his ear to spy's mouth and detected no breath. He'd been right; he'd been dragging a corpse the whole time. But Miller moved him aside and plunged his syringe into Gagarin's heart and, incredibly, the spy came back to life once again.

He was gasping more than breathing, and he couldn't move. But he was still among the living. They were all astonished he was still alive.

They carried him up to dry land and laid him out under the big Su-34, which had survived the rain of flaming debris, at least for the moment.

Hunter sprinted down the field, hoping like hell the ramp was still usable. He would have loved to see the structure in the same state as when he first saw it, but that was not to be. About a third of the planks were smoldering now, and all of them were burning around the edges. He had no time to put out these fires; there were too many of them. He ran back down the field. They had to go, right now.

He climbed back up into the airplane. Cook and Miller had already carried Gagarin into the small galley area, laying him out on a partially inflated air mattress, the only real comfort they could give him.

Hunter helped strap him in, using bungee cords and extra safety belts. Then he threw out the bloody body bag, cranked up the access ladder, and quickly started the big engines.

The Russian turbines coughed, ramped up again, but then coughed again. Not what Hunter wanted to hear, but at least they were running.

He turned back to Cook and Miller.

"Just hang on as tight as you can, guys," he said, adding, "And maybe, close your eyes."

They took his advice. Hunter didn't wait for the cabin pressure to hit the minimum; they didn't have time. He turned on the plane's nose-wheel light, boosted the throttles, and popped the brakes. Suddenly they were streaking down the bumpy and cracked runway, cutting through the rain of fire and smoke. They hit the ski jump hard, buckling a number of the weakened smoldering planks and violently shaking the plane from both ends.

At just that moment, Hunter lit the afterburners.

The next thing they knew, they were flying.

Chapter Thirty-Four

They went straight up.

Putting the big plane on its tail, Hunter booted it, the twin monster engines kicked in, and instantly they were heading right for the stars.

Streaking through the cumulus clouds of fire and smoke, they passed the circus of beleaguered Russian fighters, their pilots still waiting for an aerial attack that would never come. Up they went through sprays of tracer-laden anti-aircraft barrages and SAMs going off like fireworks displays above burning Hamburg.

Straight up . . .

At 1,200 mph . . .

Once past 35,000 feet, Hunter glanced over his shoulder to see Cook and Miller, still lying flat out on the flight deck, doing all they could to hang on to Gagarin so he wouldn't go airborne and smash into the far end of the cabin. Eyes shut in what looked like complete terror, their faces were being rippled by the onslaught of g-forces.

And still Hunter kept climbing.

Only when he reached 55,000 feet, ten miles high, did he slowly level off.

"All OK back there?" he yelled over his shoulder.

Cook and Miller couldn't talk yet; they were still trying to catch their breaths. But they each gave a thumbs-up. Then Miller checked Gagarin's vitals.

"My God, he's *still* with us," he yelled with some disbelief, adding: "But just barely."

It didn't seem possible, but the final phase of the rescue operation was about to kick in. If all went well, they would head west and meet up with Ben and JT in the loitering buddy tanker, plus its backup, somewhere over the Irish Sea. Once refueled, they would all head back to the USS *USA* together.

There was only one alteration to the plan: The goal now was to get back to the flattop while Gagarin was still alive. This meant Hunter would have to make the 1,500-mile journey at more than 1,000 mph, close to afterburner speed. That would require more aerial refuelings, and the two buddy tankers would have to keep pace with him. It was not how jet fighters usually operated; it was more like driving a car across the country at 200 mph. The engines certainly didn't like it, and if anything was going to screw-up anywhere onboard, this was the time it would pop. Especially in the less-than-perfect Su-34.

But Gagarin's condition mandated the quick dash home.

Hunter put the plane into a long, slow turn toward the west. Miller stayed with Gagarin and Cook strapped into the temporary jump seat, installed where the copilot's station used to be. This would help balance the plane in level flight.

Hunter began doing speed-to-fuel calculations when suddenly, his body began vibrating. He could feel his senses jump into overload. He gripped the plane's controls so tightly the electricity was flowing into his hands. The whir of the flight computer and the hiss of the pressurization system now sounded as loud as his two monster jet engines.

He looked over at Cook in the jump seat and said: "Sorry . . . but we've got to go back."

Cook looked at him with surprise for about two seconds, but never said a word. He unstrapped himself from the jump seat and joined Miller back in the cabin. Once again, they both lay on the floor next to the dying spy, holding onto Gagarin's straps, keeping them tight.

Hunter saw that they were as prepared as they were ever going to be. His body shaking even more so now, he pushed the nose of the big plane down and started to dive.

Sometimes, things just happen.

And something strange was happening to him right now.

He broke back through the cloud of smoke, through the skies still crowded with circling fighters and exploding anti-aircraft fire. Down to just 2,500 feet, directly over the Elbe River, about two miles north of the Kraftwerk Canal.

That's when he saw it.

Coursing its way up the Elbe, silhouetted by the fires coming from the Hamburg docks and leaving a long string of churned-up water in its wake, was the *Odessa,* Viktor's super submarine, trying to escape the firestorm by heading for the open sea.

Hunter just shook his head. His super instincts had been right.

The devil himself was nearby.

Everything made a little more sense now. The intelligence Gagarin sent back to Fitz about the end of the sun bombs could have been gleaned only from a source close to Viktor himself. This meant the super villain had to be in town, never expecting to be rained on by Fitz's furious cruise missile barrage.

It was strange, because Hunter really didn't think too much about what to do next. He had no underwing ordnance with him—but that didn't matter. His cannon was full. That's all he would need.

Reminding Cook and Miller to stay in place no matter what, he did a violent 180-degree turn and dove on the sub. He didn't even look at his fire control panel. He just let his inner self decide when to pull the trigger.

Down to just fifty feet, about a quarter mile from the stern of the fleeing submarine, he felt his finger engage the fire button.

The huge nose gun opened up in full fury. He watched as the giant cannon rounds walked right along the deck of the sub, punctuating the hull and blowing large holes in the conning tower.

Every shell seemed to hit something combustible, 105 in all. No sooner had he pulled off the strafing run, when the submarine blew up, splitting itself lengthwise from the bow to the tail fins.

Then each of the two halves blew up again. After that, the whole sad, fiery mess quickly sank into the Elbe.

It all happened in just a matter of seconds.

But finally, the Odessa Raid was complete.

Chapter Thirty-Five

It just made sense that their flight back to the USS *USA* would be marred by bad weather.

Very high winds over the Continent; rain and high seas at the carrier's present location. There was nothing Hunter could do about the atmospherics. And there was no contingency landing site. They either had to set down on the carrier or go into the sea.

They linked up with Ben and JT and a second buddy tanker, flown by Frost and Marcotte, over the south coast of Ireland. Locating them could have been a challenge in the bad conditions, but with Hunter's super-instincts and his radar, he found the two planes orbiting very close to the predetermined spot.

Hunter briefed his pilot friends on the situation aboard his plane; they understood that getting back to the carrier fast was paramount. He tanked up and stood by while Ben and JT's buddy tanker took on fuel from Frosty and Marcotte.

Then the three of them turned west, booted in their afterburners, and headed for the USS *USA*.

Hunter's Su-34 flew in the lead. But he, Cook, and Miller were forced to take shifts piloting, as they had to continuously give Gagarin chest compressions to keep his heart beating.

Hunter engaged the plane's schizophrenic autopilot system whenever it was his turn; Cook and Miller knew enough about flying that if anything drastic went wrong, they could hold the fort until he jumped back into the pilot's seat.

An extra oxygen mask provided Gagarin's ventilation between compressions. Miller had managed to stop the bleeding and clean the most horrendous of the man's wounds; welts covered most of his body. But it was clear he'd suffered many internal injuries, including a punctured lung, evident by his labored breathing, his heart, and who knew what else.

It really was astonishing the spy was *still* alive.

Gagarin remained unconscious through it all, unaware the small group of Americans was trying very hard to save him. And it seemed to go on for hours. But just as Hunter strapped himself back into the pilot's seat for the twelfth time and regained control of the airplane, he saw the electronic signature of the USS *USA* blink onto his radar screen.

They'd made the 1,000-mile journey in just under an hour, going nearly twice the speed of sound in mostly bad weather. The damage to their engines and their airplanes' frames would probably be permanent, especially with the Su-34's cranky design, and they'd burned through a lot of fuel. But they had done what they'd set out to do.

Now all that was left was to land on the carrier. In a storm. While running on fumes.

Hunter contacted the carrier immediately. He briefed them on the situation and asked that they put the emergency landing barrier across the deck. This would be a one-time attempt to get on board. His fuel was essentially gone and the buddy tankers were down to zero, too. If any of them missed trapping on the carrier the first time, doing another circuit around the boat and trying again would not be an option. They'd run out of gas first.

This had to be a one and done.

"Better double-check his belts," Hunter called back Cook and Miller. "Then strap in yourselves. This will be bumpy."

They were just two miles out now. Hunter steered the plane to starboard and began the final approach, diving through the mad torrent of rain. The wind was up to fifty knots across the deck; it was blowing the emergency barrier's phosphorous strapping in all directions. He could tell the big ship was valiantly trying to keep itself in position, so the wind was coming over the bow. But it was also being hit by gigantic waves.

At one mile out, Hunter engaged the automatic flight controls and prayed the computer's steering efforts would perfectly match his own.

At a half mile out, the wind suddenly gusted to seventy knots, nearly knocking the Su-34 over on its wing. Then they were hit by lightning.

It was just a quick flash, but it was blinding. A clap of thunder shook the plane an instant later, killing all the cockpit lights. The entire flight panel blinked once and died as well. The cabin went completely dark.

In just a few seconds, they'd lost all flight controls, all communications, all their navigation, and their cabin lights. Even their exterior emergency lights had blown out.

The curse of the Su-34 continued . . .

Hunter punched the flight control panel twice—hard. Parts of it suddenly lit back up; but half its screens stayed black. He had his attitude control and his terrain guidance module working again, but these things were basically useless for what he had to do.

The plane started dropping so quickly, there was no way any pilot could regain control and land the mortally crippled plane.

Luckily, Hunter wasn't just any pilot.

"Everyone tied down?" he yelled back to Cook and Miller. He heard two weary grunts in reply. Then he moved a lever down at his feet, giving him manual control of the plane.

The Su-34 shuddered from one end to the other with the emergency transfer of power. Hunter began flying the plane on muscles alone, pulling back on the controls with all his strength and somehow keeping them from plunging into the sea.

Fifteen hundred feet out. The carrier was just ahead, but it was battling waves the size of skyscrapers. He not only had to get to the big ship and catch the arresting wire, he had to arrive just as the ship was climbing up from the bottom of a wave. If he went in the other way, he'd drive the plane right through the flight deck.

He blew the safety charges and lowered the landing gear via a hand crank. It served to slow them down, but not by a lot.

Twelve hundred feet to go. He was gripping the controls so hard now he could feel the blood vessels in his fingers start to burst. The alarms on his partially revitalized flight board suddenly came to life, blaring klaxons throughout the cabin. One punch took care of them.

A thousand feet to go. He was guesstimating his altitude, hard to do in the midst of storm, but one thing was clear: This would not be a descent; they were going straight in—if they made it that far.

Eight hundred feet . . .

Now he could feel the tendons in his forearms start to pop. He fought to stay inside himself for just a little bit longer and let the universe guide his hands to bring them on in.

Five hundred feet . . .

Four hundred . . .

Three hundred . . .

Suddenly, Gagarin came to life. He cried out: "Dominique—my lass! We'll be together soon."

Two hundred . . .

One hundred . . .

At least he's still alive, Hunter thought soberly.

The big Su-34 slammed onto the carrier's deck a moment later. Hunter caught the two-line, but it seemed to stretch him out forever, crashing through the emergency netting and bringing the big plane right up to the edge of the deck before finally stopping.

Like having sex in a car crash. Excitement and terror in the same two seconds.

Heart pounding, he quickly killed the engines, punched the last of his emergency systems to off and disengaged the arrestor cable. Luckily he'd skidded so far he was not fouling the landing deck. He lowered the front gear door and a small army of men in Red Cross vests climbed aboard. They immediately began treating Gagarin, sticking four IV tubes into his broken arms and putting him on a stretcher, oxygen mask still attached. Hunter helped Cook and Miller get their footing on the descent ladder and safely down to the deck. Then he waited for the medics to carry out their severely wounded passenger.

As the stretcher bearers went by him, one said: "Five-star job keeping him alive. Don't worry. We got this now."

Cook and Miller helped carry the spy into the super-structure and down to the sick bay.

Seconds later, Ben and JT's buddy tanker came in for a wobbly but successful landing, also catching the two wire. Frost and Marcotte were right on their heels, snagging cable number three.

Five minutes later, all the pilots were sitting in the mess hall, downing massive amounts of coffee liberally splashed with no-name whiskey.

All except Hunter.

He was still outside taking a few moments for himself . . .

He'd walked around his Su-34, moving with the rolling, pitching deck, trying to get his mental equilibrium back to some kind of normalcy. He checked the nose of the big plane to see its front landing gear had stopped a mere two inches from the edge of the deck. A sneeze at the wrong moment during landing would have been enough to send them toppling into the ocean.

Now, he took in several deep breaths, standing alone in the hurricane of rain and wind swirling around him. Everyone had made it back alive—including Gagarin. That was the important thing. Plus, they had sunk Viktor's submarine, and the chances were extremely good that Lucifer himself was aboard when the ship went down. That was another very good thing.

A voice from deep inside whispered to him, *Mission accomplished.*

His shoulders finally loosened, his hands finally un-clenched. He took off his helmet and let the rain wash over his face. He was getting closer to home.

He turned to finally join the others in the crew mess—only to find Dominique standing behind him, waiting.

She was in a long Navy poncho, hood up, the rain and tears washing over her gorgeous face.

She came up very close to him.

"I have no words," she sputtered, looking into his eyes, beside herself with gratitude.

"None needed," he said. "He'll be OK, now that he's on board, they'll be able to. . ."

He never got the rest of his words out. She was sud-denly in his arms and kissing him deeply.

He didn't even make a token protest.

Sometimes, things just happen.

She hugged him and kissed him again.

Then she whispered in his ear: "I guess you haven't changed as much as I thought."

Chapter Thirty-Six

The next day

The Su-34's main computer—the artery-clogged heart valve on Hunter's big Russian attack plane—finally gave out just as he put the battered fighter on its final approach to the long-abandoned airport outside Sherbrook, Free Canada.

The flight from the USS *USA* had been typical. Although he'd spent several hours before taking off fixing a multitude of sins inside the jet fighter, lots of little malfunctions, lots of little gremlin attacks plagued the journey. His knuckles were scraped from punching out so many of the offending warning lights. But through it all, the main computer had hung in there, if just barely.

He'd just spotted the runway when it happened. The airstrip was lit up by hundreds of candles; he'd never seen anything so inviting.

Finally, back home.

A moment later, the entire control panel went red—and then went dead. He watched in horror as his automatic flight systems clicked off one by one.

"Really?" he asked the cosmos out loud. "You brought me this far—and *now* you're going to crap out on me?"

He delivered five well-placed punches to the spots on the control panel where a good pop would usually revive it—or part of it.

But not this time.

It was dead for good.

There was nothing he could do about it. He'd already committed to the landing and was at just 3,200 feet and coming down fast. His engines were coughing, the landing gear only halfway deployed. The oxygen system went kaput, forcing him to rip off his mask so as not to breathe in toxic fumes. When his emergency navigation beacon blinked out, he knew that was the end.

This would officially be a crash.

He slammed the steering column forward, then just as violently pulled it back in his lap. The resulting burst of residual electricity flapped his control services one more time, killing them for good. The last second maneuver raised the jet's flat nose a couple of feet just before the plane struck the runway.

The partially deployed gear hit hard and, acting like a huge spring, bounced the big fighter ten feet back into the air. It came down a second time, Hunter stomping on the backup air brakes and pushing them straight to the floor. Then came a second bounce, this one just as high and twice as violent.

The Su-34 came down again, and this time it stayed down. But it began skidding. Hunter pumped the dead air brakes twice and buried them again. They worked for a moment—but then locked and caught fire. Still he would not let up on them.

This caused more skidding. His right-wing tip disappeared in a flash. A gut-wrenching turn to the left sheared off that side's canard, creating another long stream of black smoke. The big plane was out of control and about to tip over. When that happened, what was left of the fuel inside his tanks would be ignited by his overheated brakes and he'd be blown to cinders.

Time to gamble. He took his feet off the manual brakes, eliminating that source of friction. Then he yanked the controls in the direction of the skid. It seemed to take forever, but after a few seconds, almost imperceptibly, he sensed the plane slowing down. He turned three hundred sixty degrees twice more, then, finally, the Su-34 ground to a smoky, fiery halt.

He pushed the canopy eject button. One last bit of juice caused it to blow off the top of the cockpit, allowing him to scramble out on the portside wing and jump to the ground.

There was no time to stand still and wax sentimental as the plane went through its death throes. He hustled across the runway and dove into a ditch filled with ice and snow. He covered his head and waited for the Su-34's one last fatal boom.

It dawned on him in that strange moment that he'd been doing a lot of this lately—diving for cover to avoid some huge explosion. Or trying to get out of the way of some catastrophe. On the heart-shaped island. In Hamburg. Even literally walking around in a fog for three days.

What kind of a life was he leading?

He waited a full minute, soaked, singed here and there, but still breathing.

But the explosion never came.

He put a handful of snow in his mouth to quench his thirst. Then he looked up and over the ditch and saw the Su-34 again. Incredibly, it was smoking but not burning. It was bent and twisted, and large pieces were missing, but it was still more or less intact.

"Tougher than I thought," he said aloud.

He got up and brushed the soot and dirt from his flight suit. He knew the Su-34 should have stopped working long ago. It had driven him nuts just keeping it airborne, but it had brought him home. And there was something to appreciate there, despite whose hands built it.

But he'd never get into one of them again.

He looked around, getting his bearings. Lots of trees, a runway out in the middle of nowhere. All those candles. He'd been here before. Night was just falling, but the full moon gave enough light for him to find the path that he had to take.

He began the climb up to nearby Sugar Mountain, anticipation in every step.

The lodge was just as he'd remembered it. It looked like an old tourist poster for Visit Canada, surrounded by maple and pine trees. A babbling brook, the sun setting in the background. The two-story wooden cabin was welcoming in every way.

Except—it was dark inside.

He'd been sure someone would be waiting for him.

The door was unlocked; he walked in and climbed the five stairs to the main hall. The fire was unlit, the balcony dim and lifeless.

What went wrong?

He found some matches and kindling and started a fire. No sooner did it begin crackling when he heard the door open behind him. He turned just in time to see Sara, smiling at the top of the stairs, her short blonde hair reflecting the glow of the fire. She was dressed in a sexy long white dress, low-cut, barefoot, beautiful.

She jumped with delight on seeing him.

They were embracing five seconds later. She seemed equal parts ghost and angel. He'd never really truly believed this moment would happen, certainly not while he was pining away atop the heart-shaped island. But here he was, with her again. His new-ish girlfriend. Holding her, kissing her.

"Close your eyes," she told him.

"Close my eyes?"

"Just do it," she said. "You'll thank me."

She led him through the dining room and into the kitchen, where she had a meal on the stove. Spaghetti and meatballs—his favorite.

But that was not the surprise.

"Keep them closed," she instructed him.

She brought him through the kitchen and out the back door. He knew a small aircraft barn was nearby, the road behind it led down to the other side of the airport.

Finally she made him stand still and promise to keep his eyes shut.

Then he heard her slide back the barn doors.

Finally she yelled, "OK—open!"

He did—and saw, inside the barn, a very unusual aircraft.

Delta-shaped. Six cannon barrels sticking out of its nose. Painted in his favorite colors: red, white, and blue.

Jezzus Christ . . .

It was his F-16XL—totaled during the Battle of New York.

He was dumbstruck. The last time he'd seen his beloved plane, it was a burning scrap of metal on the deck of the then Russian-controlled aircraft carrier, *Admiral Isakov*.

He just looked at her and asked.

"How?"

She came over and embraced him again. "Your friend Bull Dozer," she began. "Runs the Seventh Cavalry—now mayor of New York."

Dozer was one of Hunter's best friends. They'd fought in many battles together.

"I know him very well," he said. "My brother from a different mother,"

"Exactly," she replied with a smile. "He and his friends were able to gather up the pieces after you crashed it and put it back together. He said it was a gift to you from the City of New York."

Hunter couldn't believe it. He walked around the super-fighter; the breath catching in his throat. Never did he think he'd ever see it intact again.

"This is incredible," he said over and over.

"It gets even better," Sara told him. "Bull himself came up here when they delivered it. He told me to tell you that he's heard the Asian Mercenary Cult is evacuating the West Coast. If it's true, then America will be free of all foreign invaders for the first time since . . . well, I guess, the Big War."

That news hit Hunter with the same force as seeing his plane again. He was almost staggered.

"I need a drink," he said. "Something really strong."

Five minutes later, he was in dry clothes, stretched out on a couch, next to an outdoor fire, a soda glass filled with whiskey and ice, with Sara lying beside him. Her dress was half off. He was using a straw to ingest his drink.

This must be what happiness feels like, he caught himself thinking. They didn't really know each other very well; they'd only been an item for a couple months. But he loved being with her like this.

The booze made his head start to spin. No problem he thought. It will just make the meatballs taste better. But then the spinning got faster and suddenly he was over *Sekret Ostrov* again, and then landing on the heart-shaped island. Two slurps from his drink. Now Viktoria was whispering in his ear, and for a moment, he imagined a tiny fog bank was surrounding him.

Another two belts. Now he could feel the heat from the fires on Hamburg scorching his face again. Then he could feel Dominque's lips on his.

He took a very long swig of his drink. The glass was almost empty.

Happiness comes in threes, he thought. He was living proof of it.

He'd made it back in one piece to be with his new girlfriend. Incredibly, he had his old airplane back. And it appeared that America would truly be free again—for the first time in almost fifteen years.

Three dreams. Three dreams come true.

Deep inside he heard that voice again: "Mission accomplished."

And any other man would have just succumbed to it. Just fall into the pool of happiness and not even think about it.

But he couldn't, because something else was on his mind.

At that very moment, when he had just about everything he'd ever wanted, the question still would not go away.

Who was the girl in the baseball cap?

Coming December 10, 2019

A New Series
From Best-Selling Author
Mack Maloney

A Codename Starman Adventure
Book 1
The Kalashnikov Kiss

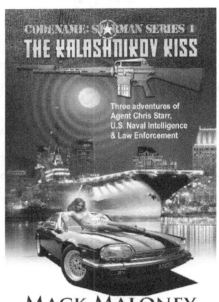

For more information
visit: www.SpeakingVolumes.com

On Sale Now!

STARHAWK *series*

For more information
visit: www.SpeakingVolumes.com

On Sale Now!

STORM BIRDS *series*

For more information
visit: www.SpeakingVolumes.com

On Sale Now!

STRIKEMASTER *series*

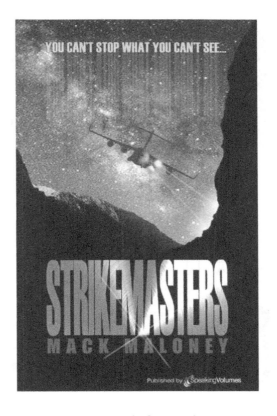

**For more information
visit:** www.SpeakingVolumes.com www.SpeakingVolumes.com

On Sale Now!

CHOPPER OPS *series*

For more information
visit: www.SpeakingVolumes.com

50% Off
Audiobooks

Made in the USA
Monee, IL
26 February 2025